MARK MY SOUL

Grayson Bell

Grayson Bell
GraysonBell.net

Cover Art by J. Pearson
lolbatty.deviantart.com

Printed in the United States of America

First Printing: 2019

ISBN: 978-1-098-79124-7

ACKNOWLEDGEMENTS

Thanks to everyone who helped me make this novel what it is. In no particular order, thank you: Roberta Blablanski, Kallin McPherson, Eric Burton, Kayla Stewart, Maria Gruber, Jennifer Moore, and Susan Wolber.

Mark My Soul would be a poorer novel without all your input and suggestions. I appreciate all your support and encouragement!

UNEXPECTED

Scott climbed out of the car and straightened his suit jacket, looking over the clean lines of the modern estate where he'd been dropped off. It was Saturday, and he was attending another *Seek Your Soulmate* party. At thirty-two, he wouldn't be expected to continue attending these much longer. *Three more years, then no one will blink an eye if I stay home on the weekends.*

Thankfully, it seemed whoever his soulmate was, she must not live in the area. Either that, or she traveled in different social circles than he did. It was just as well. The possibility of meeting his soulmate made him break out in a cold sweat and there was always one lingering worry. *What if they turn out to be a man?*

Since he still was expected to attend these parties, Scott used them as an opportunity to hookup, enjoying a different lovely lady almost every weekend. He rubbed the back of his left hand, where his soulmark was, absentmindedly. *It's better this way. I won't have to get tied down.*

The party was already well underway; music throbbed as Scott made his way through the throng of bodies on his way to the bar. He always liked to have a drink first to help him relax, since he didn't deal well with crowds of people. "Manhattan, up," he ordered once he caught the attention of the bartender.

Drink in-hand, Scott made his way to a corner of the room to better assess his options. There was a pretty brunette walking in the door and scanning the room. He contemplated making his way over to her when her face brightened into a smile, and she waved at a small cluster of other women across the room. *Ugh, no.* Women who traveled in packs were rarely hookup material, so he turned his attention elsewhere.

A young, raven-haired girl approached, drawing his attention. "Still haven't found *the one*, huh?"

"I'm looking for *the one for tonight*. Could you be her?"

"Dunno, maybe. I've always had a thing for older guys."

"Daddy kink or the appreciation of experience?"

"A little of both," she said with a wink. "I'm Emilia."

"Scott."

Taking a sip of his drink, Scott studied her for a moment. He was about to say something when his soulmark began to tingle, startling him enough that he nearly dropped his drink. "Shit!"

"What happened? Is it your mark?"

Raising his left hand he turned it over. His soulmark was clearly more pronounced, the outline becoming darker and more visible. "Yeah. Wow, I never thought that would happen tonight. It's not you, is it?"

Emilia shook her head and held up her hand. Her mark was faint and didn't match his at all. "I'm afraid not. Go get her, tiger!"

Downing his drink, Scott looked over the crowd again. He tried to spot anyone who may also be looking for their soulmate. His eyes fell on several women, but none appeared to be reacting. Scott's instinct was telling him to run for the hills, but he knew society didn't take kindly to soulmates running away from each other. *Well, I might as well have a look at her first.*

Setting his empty glass down, Scott made his way through the crowd to look through the other rooms in the house. The tingling sensation kept getting stronger, so he knew he was getting close.

As he made his way through the house, he began to imagine what his soulmate might look like. He'd always gravitated toward pretty and petite. Occasionally a handsome man would catch his eye, but he always suppressed those desires and passed them by. Same-sex soulmates were rare and came with too many societal responsibilities he would be all too happy to avoid, *thank you very much.*

Besides, Scott found himself more attracted to women. Dating women felt *safe*, and ladies seemed to enjoy his company. He'd often been told he was *sweet* and *such a gentleman.* He reasoned, why pursue male partners, when there were so many beautiful and willing ladies to be had? His soulmate was probably a woman, so there was no point exploring that side of himself. *Right?*

After searching the entire house, Scott was beginning to wonder if his soulmark was somehow broken. He nearly gave up when he saw the sliding door out to the backyard was open. Making his way outside, he saw a beautifully lit swimming pool. If the evening had been slightly warmer, no doubt there would be a bevy of party goers swimming.

The crisp night air sent a shiver through him as his eyes searched around for another living soul. Out of the shadows walked a tall, handsome man. "It's about time you came looking for me out here."

Scott's breath caught in his throat. The back of his hand began to tingle more intensely, as the man stalked his way toward him. *Oh no.*

"Hi, I'm Ross," the man introduced, reaching out.

Staring at the offered hand, with a clearly visible mark that matched his own, Scott shrank back. If he shook his soulmate's hand—if they touched skin-to-skin—it would continue the process of bonding between them. A process that was irreversible.

Flicking his eyes up to look at Ross, he shook his head. "No ... I can't do this. I'm sorry ... I just ... I can't." Turning, Scott fled back into the house, then out of the front door and down the street. He had to get out of there. Looking back, he saw that Ross wasn't running after him. He pulled out his phone and scheduled for a car to come pick him up and take him back to the city.

* * *

With shaking fingers, Scott nearly dropped his keys, as he tried to unlock the door to his apartment. Once inside, he hung his keys from a hook by the door and went to pour himself a stiff drink. *This wasn't how tonight was supposed to go.*

Collapsing onto his couch, with a glass and bottle of whiskey, he planned to drink himself into oblivion and hope he could forget this entire night had happened. After his first swallow, he startled when his phone began to vibrate in his pocket. *Who the hell is calling me at this hour?*

Fishing his phone out of his pocket he looked at the screen. *Unknown Number.* Scott dropped the phone onto the coffee table and ignored it, opting to take another long swallow of his drink. The burn of it in his throat helped make the continued tingle of his mark feel less pronounced.

The next morning, he awoke, bleary eyed. It took a few moments for him to realize he was still on the couch, a half-empty bottle of whiskey sitting on the coffee table next to his phone. Sitting up, Scott winced and rubbed at his neck. *Ugh, I'm getting too old for this.*

Purposefully ignoring his phone, he rose to start a pot of coffee before stumbling to the bathroom. After relieving himself and taking a hot shower, he began to feel almost human again. Dressed in sweatpants and a loose t-shirt, he poured himself a cup and contemplated the rest of his day. Usually he'd be having a round of morning sex or discussing breakfast options with his latest conquest. Often, he'd spend the bulk of the next day with them before parting ways. It was a pleasant way to spend a Sunday afternoon.

His soulmark's ongoing tingle began to turn into an insistent itch. It burned slightly and felt more ... urgent. Was Ross nearby, searching for him? *Fuck, I hope not.*

Draining his cup, he went to pour another when his phone buzzed. Scott stared at it for a moment before getting his refill in the kitchen. He knew who was trying to reach him and he wasn't prepared to deal with *that.* Not yet.

Leaving the phone behind, Scott made his way to the little office he had set up in the spare bedroom. He needed to do some research first. He vaguely remembered the soulmark classes he was required to take back in high school but couldn't remember all the details.

Everyone knew that such same-sex pairings were treated differently. They were so rare; they were viewed as something special. Scott needed to know if there was any way he could avoid bonding with his soulmate. He also looked up why his mark continued to itch, when he was pretty sure he hadn't touched the man he'd met last night. *Ross*, his traitorous mind reminded him.

Scott spent a couple of hours researching everything he could find on the topic. It was worse than he'd feared. Ever since he'd gotten within touching distance of Ross, his soulmark had begun to change. The proximity alone was enough to start the bonding process. However, since the physical contact hadn't occurred, the chemicals in his body were now in a disarray and his mark was becoming irritated. If he and Ross didn't complete the next stage and touch each other, the irritation would only get worse.

That also confirmed his other fears. There was no known way to reverse the bonding process safely or cure the irritation once it began. In addition, since they were a same-sex soulmate pair, he'd likely be ostracized for refusing to bond with his soulmate.

Refusal to bond happened so rarely in their society as it was, but occasionally it would come out that one or both of a pair had initially refused. However, if the pair were of the same sex, all hell broke loose. The pair would be shamed, their lives destroyed, and in some cases forced to flee into exile.

I shouldn't have run from Ross last night. Why the hell did I panic like that? Shit, this is a disaster.

While he was researching, Scott had heard his phone buzz several more times. Scratching his irritated soulmark, he sighed and resigned himself to his fate. Going back to the living room, Scott glared at his phone. Taking a deep breath, he picked it up and unlocked the home screen. There were several texts and one voicemail, all from the same unknown number.

He clicked the first text message.

Hey Scott, it's Ross. I tried to call you. The host of the party gave me your name and number. I'm sorry if meeting me freaked you out. Please, give me a call.

Scott let out a sigh of frustration. *Ugh, why does he have to sound so understanding?* Glancing back down at his phone, he read the three other texts.

Hey there. Are you awake yet? We need to talk about this.

Scott, please. Your mark must be starting to itch, too. You know what that means, right?

Scott Hansen, if you don't call me by 5pm, I'm going to come to your apartment. We need to talk.

It was 4:32pm. *Shit.*

Scott then listened to the voicemail.

"Hey, this is Ross. You know, the guy you ran away from at the party? Your soulmate? Look, I'm sorry if I wasn't what you were

expecting, but we need to talk about this, face-to-face. Now that we've activated our marks, this isn't going to go away. Please, call me."

Rubbing his face, Scott groaned. His hand shook as he clicked on the unknown number. *Come on, I can do this. It's not like I have a choice.* Taking a deep breath to steady his nerves, Scott clicked the call button and put the phone up to his ear.

"*Hello, Scott?*"

"Yeah, hi. Sorry for dragging this out. I ... needed some time to process."

"*So, let me guess, not expecting me to be a guy, right?*"

"Something like that."

"*That's a shame. I was really happy to find out you are.*"

"So, you said you wanted to talk in person? I agree ... but no touching. Not yet. Okay?"

"*Okay, but we can't wait too long to complete this part of the bonding. This irritation from our marks will only get worse.*"

"Yeah, I know. I was reading up on it before I called you."

"*Let me take you out to dinner. Meet me at 7pm at that burger dive down on Seventh.*"

"Okay, that sounds good. I'll see you there."

Rubbing his hands over his face, Scott took a deep breath. *What the hell have I gotten myself into?*

HELLO, AGAIN

Ross parked his car down the street from the diner. He chuckled to himself at the memory of his soulmate running away from him in a panic the night before. The guy was cute, from what he'd seen of him. Scott was about the same height as he was, around six-foot-one, although with a slighter build from his own muscular frame. It had been dark out, but it looked like he had sandy blond hair, which contrasted with Ross' own dark brown.

Walking toward the burger dive, Ross looked around to see if he could see Scott. It was five past seven, and he was intentionally a few minutes late. He liked to observe people he was meeting for the first time. If they didn't know he was watching them, he would be able to see a little of their authentic selves.

Looking into the window of the restaurant, Ross spotted Scott. He was already seated at a booth by one of the windows, sipping on a beer. He was fidgeting nervously with his sleeves, keeping them pulled over the back of his hands. He scratched the back of his left hand before pulling the sleeve back down. Ross could feel the echoing itch on the back of his own hand.

It made Ross' heart ache that he wasn't what Scott had been hoping for in a soulmate. It didn't make sense. *Unless, could Scott not be attracted to men?* Ross had observed him quietly as Scott was conversing with a lovely young lady before he came into range, triggering their marks. That didn't track. If they were soulmates, they had to be attracted to one another, didn't they?

Could it be because same-sex soulmates were a big deal and were subjected to a lot of media attention? Scott hadn't appeared shy, walking into that party full of confidence. *Hmm, maybe that's it. Maybe Scott had put on a front?*

Scott was checking the time again and looking increasingly agitated. Ross decided he'd better go in before his skittish soulmate would bolt again.

Entering the diner, he waved at Scott as soon as he saw him. "Hey, sorry I'm late. Traffic is getting bad around here," he fibbed as he sat across from Scott.

"It's okay. I ordered a beer while I was waiting."

The waitress came to take their order before Ross could say anything else. Once she left, Ross took a moment to study Scott's features. He did indeed have sandy blond hair, and a beautiful pair of brown eyes, the warm color of whiskey.

"Okay, so let's talk. Tell me why you ran away from me last night," Ross prompted.

"Getting right to the point, I see. I thought we already covered this ... I wasn't expecting you to be—"

"A guy?"

"Yeah. I tend to prefer my partners to be pretty and petite. I wouldn't use those words to describe you."

"No, I don't think anyone's ever called me pretty," Ross said with a wink. "But is that all it was? Are you not attracted to men? It would be a little unusual for us to be soulmates if we weren't both attracted to each other."

Scott paused and took a long pull from his beer. "Okay, I'll admit I do find some guys attractive but ... I've always avoided male partners. I remember what a big deal it was when the last local same-sex soulmate pair found each other, back when I was a kid. People still talk about them. They lost all sense of privacy."

"So, you are afraid of the loss of privacy?"

Scott nodded. "That's part of it, yeah."

He's still holding something back, Ross mused, but didn't press for more. Yet.

"You won't be going through it alone. You'll have me by your side the whole way."

"I don't even know you. Could we at least take some time to get acquainted first?"

"This irritation is going to keep getting worse, so we can't take too much time, but yeah. I'll clear my schedule for the next several days. We can hold off completing the first phase of bonding for as long as we both can tolerate it."

Scott's shoulders lost their rigid tension, almost sagging with relief. "Okay, that's great. I'd like that. I'll clear my schedule too. Oh, that reminds me. What about our host last night? You don't think she'll report that I refused to begin bonding with you, would she?"

Ross chuckled. *He's adorable when he's nervous.* "Don't worry. I didn't tell the host the real reason I wanted to contact you. I told her that you had dropped your wallet, and I wanted to return it."

"That's a relief. Thanks."

"So, anything you want to know about me?"

"Yeah, I guess. What do you do for a living?" Scott asked.

"I'm the CEO of a real estate development firm, maybe you've heard of it? Milgrave United."

"Wow, really? Wait are you ... Ross Milgrave? Like ... *the* Ross Milgrave?"

"The one and the same," Ross admitted, before lowering his voice. "Don't go shouting it out too loudly, please."

"Oh, yeah, sorry."

"So, how about you, Scott? What do you do?"

"I'm only a novelist. I'm currently working on my next book."

Interesting. That will make it easy to keep him at home, Ross thought. "I thought your name sounded familiar," Ross said. "You wrote *The Conspiracy Murders*, didn't you?"

Scott's eyes went wide. "You've read my books?"

"Yeah," Ross admitted with a smirk. "I read whenever I have some spare time. I really enjoyed your writing."

Seeing Scott's features turn rosy at the compliment made Ross smile. *Perfect. He responds well to praise. How adorable.*

They spent the next hour talking. Ross kept a close eye on Scott's mannerisms as they spoke. He was beginning to see why they were soulmates. Scott easily let Ross dominate the conversation, and instinctually kept his head lowered, both signs that he had some deep-seated submissive tendencies. That piqued Ross' interest, and by the end of their meal he couldn't wait to get his hands all over Scott.

"Scott, please look at me," Ross commanded. Once Scott's eyes flicked up, trying hard to hold his gaze although it was clear it made him uncomfortable, Ross spoke. "I'd like to draw up an agenda for us this week. I know you'd probably like for us to get to know each other more organically, but we don't have the time for that. For both our sakes."

Scott frowned for a moment, before scratching at the same itch Ross was feeling in his mark. Sighing in resignation, Scott nodded. "Yeah, okay."

Ross smiled. By the end of the week he'd have Scott eating out of his hand, figuratively speaking. *Hmm, and maybe literally.*

* * *

Once he was home, the first thing Ross did was sit down and plan out the rest of the week. It was clear that Scott had repressed his attraction to men for a long time, so he knew he'd have to go easy on him at first.

Since Scott was so skittish, Ross decided not to tell him everything about his own personal *proclivities*, yet. It was clear to him that his soulmate was naturally submissive, along with being bisexual. Scott seemed to have repressed one, if not both, parts of himself. It was up to Ross to make him feel at ease and unashamed of that. The key would be to figure out why he had bottled them up in the first place.

Although, if he'd only dated demure women, he may not even be aware of his submissive side.

Ross worried it would take longer to make Scott comfortable than they would have time for. The irritation on his mark was growing steadily and it would become unbearable within a few days.

Looking down at his soulmark, Ross sat back and wondered about this strange phenomenon of human biology. It wasn't unusual for two soulmates to never meet. About twenty percent of the population never did. They were known as unbonded and many of them would settle for another unbonded partner. He had never heard of a soulmate pair who had met and didn't eventually bond. It was unheard of.

Once you were within about twenty feet of your soulmate, the marks would somehow detect each other and activate the first stage of the bonding process.

As soon as the pair touched, through a handshake, a hug, or even a kiss, that would complete the first stage of bonding and begin changing their body chemistries. Science didn't completely explain why, but it seemed to have something to do with genetic compatibility. Obviously, this was irrelevant when it came to same-sex soulmates, but it was believed that having some homosexual couples brought a certain stability to society that otherwise might not be there.

The bonding process concluded when the pair consummated their relationship. At that point they would be bonded for life, their body chemistries uniquely attuned to each other. Ross didn't pretend to understand all the biology behind it, but he knew that now that he had met Scott, there was no way to reverse the process. It had begun, and they would have to see it through.

Once Ross finalized the itinerary for the week, he double checked his calendar and sent a note to his personal assistant to reschedule the meetings he'd planned that week. All his attention needed to be on Scott and convincing his handsome soulmate to bond with him—sooner rather than later.

DESPERATION

Scott checked his phone early the next morning and saw an email from Ross. Immediately a lump formed in his throat. He wanted to ignore the email, but he didn't have much of a choice. Opening the attachment, he saw it was the itinerary that Ross had promised to send him. The first item was to meet Ross for brunch that morning. Checking his clock, he was relieved he still had a couple of hours before he had to be there.

Meeting Ross yesterday had been—*interesting*. The man exuded self-assurance. Scott worked hard to display a certain level of confidence but was always second-guessing himself. In truth, he was filled with insecurity and rarely let anyone get close enough to see that side of him. Scott was afraid there was no way to hide that from Ross.

Getting up to make some coffee, Scott wondered why he had agreed so willingly to all of Ross' suggestions. He normally wasn't a pushover, but there was something about the man's quiet dominance that brooked no argument. Maybe it was the knowledge that Ross was his soulmate, but he had found himself readily agreeing, despite his initial attempt to flee his fate the other night.

Coffee in-hand, he plunked down on the couch and read through the rest of the itinerary. Every day was filled with various activities. Shared meals, movies, hikes, picnics. Everything seemed ordinary and almost banal. Typical first date activities of the unbonded. The final activity made him raise his eyebrows. *Spend the night together.*

Despite the inevitability of that, it still took Scott off-guard. He'd been trying to ignore the fact that he would, in fact, have sex with Ross at some point. Their biology demanded it. Scott wasn't necessarily opposed to the idea but going through with it was an entirely other matter.

Allowing himself to admit that he had an attraction to men was pushing himself outside of his comfort zone. The mere fleeting thought of touching Ross made his heart race and his throat tighten. He struggled to catch his breath and calm down.

What the hell is wrong with me? Ross seems kind, plus he is good-looking and successful. Why does the mere thought of being with him keep driving me into a blind panic?

Still conflicted over everything, Scott got up and began to pace. The thought of being stuck with Ross for the rest of his life still terrified him. This wasn't how meeting your soulmate was supposed to work. There should be instant chemistry. Love at first sight. Not fear and anxiety.

Scott wasn't even sure why the thought of being with Ross scared him so much, but the more he thought about it, the worse his anxiety became. He sat back down and went online to do another last-ditch search. *How do I reverse a soulmark bond?*

Digging deeper than he had the last time, he came across a link that looked like it had some possibility: *Is your soulmate not what you expected? Need to reverse the bonding process? Try our new unbonding formula! 100% natural! Results guaranteed!*

It should be suspicious that this was buried so deep on the internet, but Scott clicked on the link without giving it any thought. After reading through the page and several positive testimonials, Scott's heart rate sped up. He wasn't the only one going through this!

He didn't have much time—it claimed it was most effective if used before the initial bonding touch occurred. He placed an order and selected the ridiculously overpriced cost of overnight shipping.

He didn't want to raise Ross' suspicions, so he'd go through with their itinerary today. If they never touched, he could take this remedy tomorrow and hopefully be free of the growing irritation and reset his mark.

Then, all he'd have to do is leave town. Thankfully, as a writer he could work on his novels from anywhere. So, he decided to book a flight to the Caribbean. A little resort on the beach would be exactly what he'd need to get back into the groove again.

Once that was accomplished, Scott felt his stress ease. After finishing his coffee, he went to take a shower and dress. He could put up with Ross for one more day before leaving him behind forever.

* * *

Fiddling with his tie, Scott stared at the restaurant Ross had asked to meet him at. It was much fancier than the burger dive they had met at the day before. *Might as well get this over with.*

Making his way inside and giving his name, the hostess immediately led him to a table. "Mr. Milgrave will join you shortly. He called to say he'd be a few moments late."

"Uh, thanks."

It seemed that Ross liked to be *fashionably late*. Scott wondered if that was on purpose or habitual. Shrugging to himself, he perused the menu in front of him. He often skipped breakfast and normally didn't do brunch, so there were items on the menu he wasn't familiar with.

As he was trying to decide between the eggs benedict and the fancy sounding breakfast burrito, Ross arrived. "Good morning. I see you have a penchant for being punctual."

"Yeah, and you seem to like running late," Scott observed.

"Guilty as charged!" Ross admitted with an easy laugh, before taking the menu out of Scott's hands. "This is one of my favorite places for brunch. If you don't mind, I'll order for both of us?"

Taking a deep breath, Scott shrugged. "Okay. I wasn't sure what I wanted, anyway." *There I go, letting him take control again. What's up with that?*

Ross ordered the eggs benedict for them both, along with the restaurant's signature hash browns, coffee, and mimosas. "You'll love it, trust me."

"You like to be in control, don't you?"

"Ah, you found me out. Does that bother you?"

Scott shrugged again. "Not sure. I've always been the independent, loner type. I hope that doesn't bother you."

"We're soulmates. I'm sure we'll find the right balance."

Yeah, not if I have anything to say about it.

When the food arrived, Scott agreed begrudgingly that everything was delicious. Watching Ross as they ate, Scott could see that he had impeccable table manners. That made him feel self-conscious of his own. He had never gotten down the more refined ways of eating. He wasn't a cave man by any means, but Ross put his own etiquette to shame.

After brunch, he and Ross took a walk to a local park. Scott made sure to keep his hands buried in his jacket pockets to avoid Ross attempting to hold hands.

"So, are you currently working on a novel?" Ross asked.

"I finished my latest manuscript last week. It's with my publisher now, so I'm between projects."

"What's it about?"

"Another murder mystery," Scott said with a dismissive shrug. "What about you? What sort of real estate are you currently developing?"

"You know the new high-rise that's been going up downtown? That's my company's current project."

"Wow. That building is impressive. I've been by there a few times on my way to my publisher's office."

"Yeah, it's the biggest one we've done so far. So, any ideas for your next book?"

"I always have some ideas percolating, but I need to take a break before I start in on the next one. My publisher won't pester me for at least a month."

They spent the rest of the afternoon wandering around town and then took in a movie before having dinner. Scott felt himself begin to relax around Ross and realized he was enjoying the man's company. The fact that Ross never once brought up their soulmarks or tried to touch him was reassuring.

Still, Scott had this itch under his skin and looked forward to being alone again. He had become a novelist primarily out of his own need for personal space. Which is why all the endless parties he had been attending had gotten tedious, despite the pleasurable company he'd often managed to bring home with him for a night.

As soon as Scott made it back to his apartment, he began packing. They had no plans to meet up again until the following afternoon. That should give him time to take the remedy and get to the airport before Ross ever suspected anything.

Scott decided to write Ross a "Dear John" email and scheduled for it to send at the same time his flight was to take off. That was about two hours before he and Ross had agreed to meet next. By then there would be nothing Ross could do about it. With all his plans in place and his bags packed, Scott went to sleep. He could only hope that his order would arrive on time tomorrow.

* * *

The next morning Scott was woken up by the delivery service. He rang them into his building and eagerly grabbed the package when they arrived at his apartment door. Scott was feeling generous and handed the man a twenty-dollar tip for his promptness.

Eagerness aside, Scott decided to hold off taking the remedy, waiting until he was about to leave for the airport. He was afraid that Ross' mark might also react to the change and alert him to something being wrong. The last thing he needed was Ross barging in on him right now.

Instead, Scott took a leisurely shower, before double-checking that he'd packed everything he'd need for his trip. His phone had his boarding pass and resort reservations. He could already imagine himself sitting beach-side with his laptop, typing away.

Once he was dressed, he had plenty of time for a final pot of coffee before heading out. While the coffee brewed, he set his suitcase by the door. Then he grabbed a cup and flipped through the channels on his TV while he sipped. He'd finished a couple of cups when it was almost time for his taxi to arrive. He turned off the TV and began pacing, glancing at the bottle that sat on the kitchen counter several times. When he checked his watch again, he decided it was now or never.

Grabbing the bottle, he headed toward the bathroom. Just in case this made him violently ill, he wanted to be close to the toilet. He read the label one more time before unscrewing the cap. The instructions said to drink the bottle all in one go as quick as possible.

Looking at himself in the mirror he unscrewed the bottle. *Well, here goes nothing.*

TAKING CONTROL

Ross paced in his study. The irritation in his hand was getting worse, and he wasn't sure if he could restrain from touching Scott the next time they met. Holding back the day before had been torture, but it was worth it to see Scott finally relax around him.

Still, something felt off today and he had a strong urge to run over to Scott's apartment and pull him into an embrace, consensual or not. *No, no. Bad idea. That will just spook Scott more.*

Today he'd planned another relaxed day of activities, starting with an afternoon picnic before taking in a play at the local theater. Finally, they'd end the evening with a late dinner. Ross had been hopeful that Scott would continue to relax in his company and maybe allow some skin contact. Even holding hands would be enough, and the mere thought put a knot of emotion into Ross' chest.

It was still a few hours before their picnic, and Ross was feeling more antsy by the moment. This wasn't like him to feel anxious. *What the hell is wrong with me?*

As that thought crossed his mind, Ross fell to his knees with a scream. The irritation in his mark flared into a bright, searing pain. Something was wrong. *Very wrong.* They should still have several days before their marks would begin to react like this.

Everything Ross read said it would be a slow buildup that took nearly a week, not a sudden, blinding burst of agony.

Something must have happened to Scott. Ross picked up his phone and tried to call him, but as usual there was no response. Frustrated, he shoved his phone back into his pocket and stood, cradling his hand as he went to grab his keys. He had to get to Scott, now.

* * *

Arriving at Scott's apartment building, Ross parked his car and hurried inside. He rang Scott's apartment number. Once again, no response. Frantically Ross began ringing other apartments until someone buzzed him through.

Once he was in the elevator, Ross slumped against the back corner, cradling his hand. He hoped Scott was okay and hadn't done something desperate. It felt like hours when the elevator dinged and opened at the fifth floor. Ross practically stumbled out and made his way down the hall. He was about to bang on the door marked 528 when he saw it was slightly ajar. *Shit.*

Pushing the door open, he found Scott collapsed on the floor, a suitcase lying next to him. "Scott! What have you done?" Kneeling, he reached out to check for a pulse. "I'm sorry. I know you can't consent, but I need to know."

Ross sighed in relief when his fingers pressed against Scott's neck and felt the steady rhythm of his pulse. The pain in his hand also eased although it didn't go away. At least the first phase of the bonding process was now complete. This was hardly the romantic way he'd hoped to do it, but Ross was relieved it was done.

Unfortunately, he was sure that Scott would be less than thrilled, but what choice did he have? Ross eyed the suitcase with disdain. *Where the hell were you running off to?*

Shaking Scott, he tried to wake him. "Hey, Scott, wake up!"

No response. Sighing, Ross closed the apartment door and stooped to pick Scott up, carrying him to the sofa. Once he'd laid him down, he decided to make a quick search.

He found the bottle in the bathroom trashcan. It contained some vile smelling *remedy* that promised to break a soulmate bond. *Fuck.* Just when Ross thought he'd started to get through to Scott. Instead his soulmate had tried to break the tentative bond they'd already formed and run off to who-knows-where. That was simply not acceptable.

Ross knew he should call an ambulance, but his reputation was at stake. If this came to light, they might both be publicly shamed and possibly ostracized. It would be disastrous for his business. He was less worried for himself, and more worried for all his employees. So, instead he dialed his private physician's number.

"Hey Doc, it's Ross. I have a situation where I need the utmost discretion. Can you meet me at this address ASAP?" Ross relayed the address and ended the call. Hopefully they could keep this out of the media.

It was clear that his slow and careful approach with Scott was a complete failure. Ross decided he would need to change tactics and take Scott in-hand before this entire situation completely unraveled.

Sitting down on the coffee table, he looked at his unconscious soulmate. "Why are you so scared of me, Scott?"

Since he'd already touched him once, there was no longer any harm in doing so again. Ross reached out and took Scott's left hand in his. He traced his thumb over the now more prominent soulmark. His own was still throbbing, but not nearly as much as before. Whatever was in that *remedy* was trying its damnedest to break their bond. He could only hope that continuing to touch Scott would help counteract it somehow.

Ross was still waiting for the doctor to arrive when his phone buzzed in his pocket. Reaching for it, he took a quick look and his heart nearly stopped when he saw an email from Scott pop into his notifications. Clicking on it, his eyes kept flicking to Scott's passive face as he read over the words.

Ross,

By the time you read this, I should be boarding my flight. I'm sorry to do this to you, but I just can't be with you. I can't explain why. I don't really understand it myself, but the idea of spending my life with you terrifies me.

If you feel any changes in your soulmark, it's because I took a remedy that is meant to reset my body chemistry and break the bonding process between us.

You seem like a good guy, and I hope one day you find someone who is worthy of you. Please, don't try to find me.

Scott

Staring at his phone, Ross felt a tear trickle down his face. Scott had planned on running again. This time for good. Looking over at Scott, emotions warred inside of him. He had come close to losing the man today, losing the soulmate he'd been searching so hard to find. "Scott, what in the world could make you this terrified of being with me?"

When the door chime sounded, Ross startled. He wiped his face and stood, going to the apartment door to push the button and ring in who he hoped was his doctor. It was worrisome that Scott was still unconscious, although Ross hoped it was a good sign that the pain in his hand was slowly fading. Moments later a knock on the door brought Ross out of his reverie.

"Hey, Doc. Glad you could make it on such short notice."

"You said this was urgent and required discretion? What's going on?"

Ross explained the situation and handed the empty bottle to the doctor. "Oh my. This is bad. I've heard of these quacks. This remedy wreaks havoc on the nervous system as it attempts to reset the chemical balance in the body back to a state before the soulmark was activated. Sometimes it works, but often it can damage the entire lymphatic system. It's even led to a few deaths."

"Fuck, that's bad. Scott's been unconscious since I found him. Is there anything we can do? I'd like to keep this out of the press, if possible. You know what it would do to my reputation if this came out."

"So, he's your soulmate? Why would he be so foolish as to want to break his bond with you?"

"I have no idea, Doc. He's been skittish about this ever since we met last weekend. He ran as soon as he realized I was a man.

I had to track him down and I've been trying to get him to warm up to me. It's been an uphill battle, as you can see."

"Well, the first thing we need to do is empty his stomach," the doctor said as he set down the bag he was carrying. Pulling out a bottle from his bag, he handed it to Ross. *Ipecac.* "We need to get him to drink this and then get him over a sink or toilet quickly."

"Okay. I can carry him to the kitchen. Follow me."

Ross picked Scott up again and carried him over into the small kitchen. The doctor followed while Ross set Scott down onto his feet as best as he could. "Hold his head back and open his mouth," the doctor instructed. He then poured the Ipecac into Scott's mouth and rubbed his throat to get him to swallow. Once it was down, Ross tilted Scott upright and bent him over the kitchen sink.

It took a few moments until Scott's body began to heave, and the contents of his stomach spewed into the sink. Ross ran the faucet to help flush it down as more kept coming up. Only once Scott was dry heaving, his stomach finally empty, did Ross see fit to breathe. He wiped Scott's face clean as gently as possible and then carried him back to the couch.

"Okay, now what?"

"Now, let's try to get him to drink some water, and a couple of these tablets," the doctor instructed. "They should help counteract the effects of whatever is still left in his system. He should also receive as much skin-to-skin contact from you as possible. Touch from his soulmate can help bring his body chemistry back to where it should be. If we got to him in time, then the damage should be minimal."

Filling a glass of water and bringing it back over to Scott, Ross asked. "Is it a good sign that the pain in my own mark has started to recede?"

"It has? Yes, that is a very good sign."

"I think I'd like to move him back to my place, so I can keep a closer eye on him. Is it safe to move him?"

"It should be, yes."

"Then help me grab his suitcase, and I'll carry him down to my car."

The doctor didn't ask why Scott had a packed suitcase ready to go. Ross looked around and found Scott's keys. Lifting the unconscious man again, he carried him out of the apartment and let the doctor lock the door and follow him downstairs. Thankfully, they didn't encounter anyone in the elevator on the way down.

Once Scott was secured in Ross' car with Scott's belongings in the back seat, he bid the doctor goodbye. The doctor promised to stop by tomorrow. Then Ross was off, wanting to get Scott to his home as quickly as possible.

COMING TO TERMS

Scott woke with a groan. Every part of his body throbbed with a dull ache. It took him a moment to remember the last thing that happened. *His soulmark.* Moments after he had downed that bottle of supposed unbonding *remedy*, his soulmark had begun to sear into his hand like a live brand. After that he couldn't remember anything.

The next thing he realized was that he felt a warm body snuggled around him. *What the hell?* His eyes flew open to see Ross's head tucked into his shoulder, while the rest of him was curled around him. *Oh no, he's touching me!* Ross had promised not to touch him without his consent.

Now he was curled around him and they were both naked. What else could Ross have done while he was unconscious? Trying to reach behind him, Scott tentatively touched his anus. It didn't feel sore or abused in any way.

Okay, so I don't think I was raped. Still, what the hell happened? I was supposed to be in the Caribbean by now. Fuck! What a mess.

When he slowly tried to extricate himself from Ross, Scott realized his left ankle was caught on something. Sitting up he pulled back the blanket to see why he was stuck. That's when he saw that his ankle was chained to the foot of the bed.

Ross chained me up?! Shoving at Ross, Scott had about enough. "Hey, what the hell is the meaning of this!?"

Ross blinked the sleep from his eyes before scowling at him. "Oh, you're finally awake. It took you long enough."

"Why the hell am I chained, *naked* to ... what!? *Your bed!?* What happened to your promise of not touching me!? You kidnapped me! I can't believe I get an ass like you for a soulmate!"

Ross growled and sat up. "Now see here, if anyone's been an ass..." Ross paused and took a breath. "This isn't how I wanted for any of this to go."

"There is no way you can explain why you violated my consent! How can I be sure you didn't try to rape me while I was unconscious!?"

"There damned well is a good explanation. First, let's get one thing clear, I had no choice. I had to maximize our skin-to-skin contact or you might have died. Second, I never attempted to rape you or consummate our bond. Look at your mark if you don't believe me," Ross said.

Looking at his left hand, Scott saw that Ross was telling the truth. His mark wasn't fully defined yet.

"I knew something was wrong the moment my mark flared with searing pain," Ross continued. "I tried to call, and when you didn't pick up, I came over to your place. Your door was unlocked, and you were lying on the floor. I ... for a moment I thought you were dead." An anguished look flitted over Ross' face. "I had to check and see if you had a pulse. I couldn't do that without touching you."

"Oh ... but—"

"Yeah, *oh*," Ross growled again. "No buts. Thinking you might be dead, and the pain in my hand kept getting worse. I didn't understand why ... until I found that bottle."

"You went through my apartment?"

"Yes, I damn well searched your place. I had to know why you were passed out. Then I called my doctor, and he came over and helped me empty your stomach and gave me some medication to stabilize your body chemistry," Ross explained. "Unfortunately, that alone wasn't going to be enough, after what you had done. He said I had to make skin-to-skin contact with you as much as possible. So, for over a day I've been cuddling with you almost non-stop."

"Over *a day*?" Scott groaned. "I was unconscious for over a day!? *Shit*!"

"Yeah, shit indeed. You nearly *died* on me. Not to mention that you were planning to run off to who-knows-where! I guess I can at least be grateful you sent me an email instead of merely disappearing."

Scott sat in stunned silence for a moment, feeling thoroughly chastised. "Is that why you chained me up?"

"Yes, that's *exactly* why. I know this whole having a man as your soulmate thing is freaking you out, but that's no reason for you to risk your life trying to get away from me. At the very least you owe me an explanation. *I need to know why.*"

Scott buried his face in his hands. "I don't know why. All I know is the very thought of being with you scares the shit out of me. It has from the first moment I saw you. I thought this whole soulmate thing was meant to be all sunshine and rainbows, but for me it's been nothing but a nightmare."

"Really? So, the time we spent together was *that* bad?"

"Well … *no*. Once we got to talking, I realized you weren't a bad guy. You're easy to talk to and we get along well. I don't understand my reaction any more than you do."

"I had a feeling you might say that. I've had time to think about this, and I have some ideas. We have some time before we'll need to consummate the bond now that we've completed the touching phase. Are you willing to see this through with me?"

Scott took another deep breath. That damned *remedy* nearly killed him, and now that this phase of bonding was complete, there wasn't any turning back. Breaking the bond now would certainly kill him and could hurt or kill Ross as well. Despite his anxiety over the situation, Scott didn't want to take the risk of either himself or Ross coming to harm.

Slowly nodding, Scott agreed. "Okay. I'll see it through this time. It's not like I really have a choice now."

Sighing with relief, Ross wrapped his arms around him. "Thank you. Promise me, if you feel like running again, tell me first? We need to work through this together."

The feeling of Ross' arms holding him was more comforting than he'd expected, and Scott leaned into the touch. He wrapped his own arms around Ross for a moment before pushing back to look at him.

"I'll try," Scott promised. "So, what now?"

"Okay, first off, I'd like you to stay at my house for a few days while we work through some things. I'll unchain you, but if you do try to run again, I will keep you under lock and key next time."

A shiver went through Scott at those words. He wasn't sure why, but they made him want to obey. *Why did my cock twitch at that thought?* "Alright. I was planning on being away for a while. This isn't quite the Caribbean vacation I had envisioned, but I guess it'll do."

Ross smiled at him. "Good. Do you feel up to showering and having some breakfast? I can whip up something for the two of us."

"Yeah. I ache all over. I think a hot shower would do me some good."

Ross got up and unlocked the cuff around Scott's ankle. "Your clothes are hanging in the closet. Come meet me in the kitchen downstairs when you're ready."

"My clothes?"

"You had a packed suitcase when I found you. I brought it with."

"Oh yeah, that's right. Thanks."

Scott got up as Ross slipped on some sweatpants and left. He made his way over to the large bay window that overlooked ... well it looked like an estate. There was a large swimming pool, manicured lawns, and a beautiful flower garden. Surrounding it were dense woods as far as his eyes could see. He knew Ross was wealthy, but this blew him away.

Looking around, he located the closet and the en suite bathroom. It was huge, with a large two-person shower and an equally large soaker tub. Everything was tiled in marble. *Okay, I could get used to living like this.*

The shower had so many water heads, it confused him for a moment until he figured out the controls. Once he stepped into the spray, it was heavenly. The hot water helped soothe the ache in his body. It seemed like he would never run out of hot water, so he stayed until his fingers began to prune.

He found his clothes in the enormous walk-in closet, along with the suitcase he'd packed for his trip. Sighing, he shook his head. *What the hell was I thinking, trying a stunt like that? It seemed like such a good idea at the time, but who am I kidding? I can't fight my own biology.*

After dressing in a pair of his comfiest jeans and a t-shirt he went back to the bathroom to brush his teeth and shave. Feeling almost human again, he made his way out of the bedroom and found his way downstairs. He followed the smell of coffee until he found the unnecessarily large kitchen. "Wow, this is some place you have here."

"Thanks. A perk of my profession. Normally, I have staff to help, but I gave them the week off. I wanted to keep everything between us for now. The fewer people who know, the better. You know what would happen if people find out one of us rejected our soulmate bond. It could ruin both of us."

A rush of guilt overcame Scott as his faced heated with shame. "Yeah, I guess I hadn't thought of that when I was making my plans. I'm sorry."

"We'll work on that. For now, let's have breakfast. How do you take your coffee?"

"Black, thanks. What do you mean *we'll work on that?*"

"You'll see. It'll be easier to explain if I can show you what I mean. I have some special equipment and techniques that might help."

Scott was skeptical, but he shrugged and sipped the cup of coffee that Ross handed him. "Mmm. This coffee is good."

"I'm glad you like it. It's my favorite blend."

* * *

After breakfast, Ross led Scott into his study. "Please, sit. We need to talk first because I don't want to spook you again."

His heart rate sped up as Scott sat in one of the leather wingback chairs that Ross indicated, while Ross sat in the chair opposite. "You do realize when you say things like that, it starts me feeling anxious, right?"

"Hmm, no. I didn't realize that. Thank you for telling me. Please, if I do or say anything that triggers you again, tell me. We need to learn how to communicate with each other if this is going to work."

Nodding, Scott agreed.

Ross looked at him thoughtfully for a moment. "Now, tell me, how much do you know about BDSM?"

KINKY PROPOSITIONS

Ross sat back and watched Scott's expression. There was a mix of understanding, apprehension, and definite interest there.

"Um, well ... I've heard about it. BDSM I mean. I know it stands for bondage, domination, sadism, and masochism. Right?"

"That's exactly right," Ross replied. "So, do you have a basic understanding of what it means for people to engage in dominance and submission?"

"I think so?" Scott replied sounding less sure. "It's like one partner is dominant and takes charge, and the submissive lets them?"

Oh, he's practically a blank slate. Perfect.

Ross smiled, restraining his more feral instincts. "Well, yes and no. That's an oversimplified way to look at it," Ross started to explain. "First, I need you to know that I've always been the dominant in my relationships. I have a weakness for submissive partners."

Giving Scott a moment to process that information, Ross got up. "Wait here for a moment."

Ross made his way to the kitchen and brewed a fresh pot of coffee. When it was finished, he grabbed the pot and two mugs, and brought them back to the study. Pouring two cups and handing one to Scott, he sat back down. He smirked at the slightly stunned look that was still on Scott's face. "Tell me what you're thinking."

"I ... um..." Scott hesitated as a red flush bloomed across his face. "I'm picturing myself on my knees, tied up, while you're beating me black and blue."

Seeing in his mind's eye a very naked Scott on his knees made Ross' cock twitch. *Oh, you have no idea what I want to do to you.*

"Scott, let me first reassure you that I will never do anything that would harm you, and never anything without your consent," Ross said, pleased when Scott relaxed into his chair. *Good.* "The last thing I want is for you to be afraid of me, okay?"

"Yeah ... okay. But ... well, I've never been into that kind of stuff. What if I never am?" Scott asked before taking a sip of his coffee.

"I have practiced BDSM for most of my adult life, and it's something I would prefer not to give up. However, if you ultimately decide it's not for you, I cannot in good conscience force you," Ross admitted.

Scott looked like he was going to say something, so Ross raised a hand. "Please, let me finish," Ross said, and Scott once again relaxed back into the chair at his request. *Yes, good boy.*

"Let me get right to the point. Scott, you show clear signs of being a submissive, and I think there are some BDSM practices that could help you learn to relax and not be so anxious. I'm hoping that, besides being my soulmate, that you may also consider becoming my sub."

A look of terror flitted over Scott's face for a moment, before he sucked in several deep breaths. He relaxed his features into a look of resignation. "You think I might relax if you whip me into submission?"

Oh, you have so much to learn. Please, let me get you there.

Ross shook his head, chuckling. "No, not at all. I won't deny that I enjoy impact play, but as I said, I would never use it to force anyone into submission. That's not how BDSM works," Ross explained. "Now, take a deep breath, and please don't jump to conclusions until you hear me out."

Scott took several deep breaths before nodding. "Okay."

"Good boy," Ross said, pleased at Scott's reaction to the praise. The tension in his body immediately seemed to ease, and the lines between his eyes softened.

"See what I mean about being a natural submissive? You follow my directions so easily. I think allowing yourself to submit to me would be one step toward helping with whatever keeps sending you into a panic," Ross explained. "Today, I only want to talk, but first I need you to go over a comprehensive list of BDSM practices, so we can discuss where your limits are. I need to know what things you would be willing to try, what things you are less sure about, and what things are a definite no. Understanding your limits is important for me. I don't want to further traumatize you."

"Okay, then what is the goal of all this?" Scott questioned.

"Initially, to help you let go of some of your fear, especially concerning the two of us. Later, my goal would be to have fun and enjoy each other. Other goals may arise as we get to know each other better. I suspect that since we're soulmates, our interests and limits will be fairly compatible."

"Will you tell me what yours are?" Scott asked.

"Yes, of course, but not before you go through a list and we've discussed what your limits are. I don't want you to change your preferences based on what I like."

Scott nodded. "Okay, that sounds fair."

"Excellent," Ross said as he got up and went over to the large desk that sat at one end of the room. He pulled out some paper and brought a pen. "Here's the list. I'm going to leave you alone with it, so you can consider it all privately and don't feel like I'm hovering. If you have questions, mark them with a question mark and we can discuss those later. I'll check back with you in an hour or so. If you need anything, there's an intercom on the wall behind the desk you can use."

"Alright, thanks."

* * *

Making his way back to the master suite, Ross took some time to take a shower and change into something less casual than sweatpants. He knew it was important to show Scott he still trusted him, but in case he tried to run again the security system on his estate was fully armed. If Scott tried to go outside, it would be triggered, and Ross would be immediately notified.

Once dressed, he made his way back to the kitchen to fix them some lunch. This would be a stressful day for Scott, so some comfort food was in order. Ross hoped that Scott enjoyed grilled cheese sandwiches as much as he did.

While he cooked, Ross thought back on some of his earlier relationships. He had made plenty of mistakes along the way in his exploration of his own sexuality and kinks. In some ways, going through those experiences may have helped prepare him to become the kind of Dom Scott would need in his life. *I hope so, for both our sakes.*

The first sub that Ross had been with was a needy, skittish thing, not unlike Scott in some ways. Ross winced to himself as he recalled how royally he screwed that relationship up.

Ross had recently discovered his desire to dominate a partner when he'd met the young man. Todd had been completely smitten with Ross. Since Todd wasn't entirely new to the scene, Ross had assumed that Todd would know when to use his safeword. Their first scene had been a disaster, ending with Todd curled in a fetal position, crying hysterically. Ross hadn't known to check in on his sub periodically during a scene and hadn't realized he'd gone past Todd's limits with a cane, until Todd collapsed in a crying heap.

I do hope he forgave me. I was such an idiot back then.

Piling each grilled cheese sandwich as he completed it onto a plate, he re-examined how he'd been with Scott so far. *I can't screw this up. Not this time. He's my soulmate. I must make this work. He responds to me so easily, just like Todd did, but...*

Ross took a deep breath and blinked, seeing a cloud of black smoke rising from the pan he'd been making the sandwiches in. "Shit!" he cried out as he took the pan off the stove and turned off the burner. *Well, that's what I get for not paying attention. Alright universe, I get the message.*

* * *

Once Ross cleaned up the mess, he made his way back to the study with the unburnt sandwiches. Scott sat in the wingback chair, hunched over, his brow furrowed, as he studied the document. "Do you have questions?" Ross asked as he set down the plate on the table next to Scott.

"Yeah … I have a *lot* of questions. I don't know what half of this stuff means."

Ross chuckled with amusement. "I had a feeling that would be the case. I made us some lunch. Let me go put another pot of coffee on, and then we can talk."

Smiling to himself, Ross went back to the kitchen with the empty pot of coffee. The way Scott had been staring so intently at the list was endearing. Since bringing Scott home with him, Ross had plenty of time to think while he'd held his unconscious soulmate in his arms. He'd imagined this scenario in his mind so many times. *I was afraid Scott would try to run off again right away. He'd scared me with that stunt he pulled, but I can see he's trying to make this work. Fuck, who am I kidding? We both need to make this work.*

After Ross came back to the study with the coffee, he was pleased to see half of the sandwiches were already gone. "Well, at least you like my cooking," Ross observed as he poured them each another cup.

"Yeah, these are great. Grilled cheese is one of my favorites. How'd you know?" Scott asked.

Shrugging Ross sat down and grabbed a sandwich for himself. "I didn't. They're also a favorite of mine, and I thought today we could both use some comfort food."

"Yeah," Scott agreed. "So, how should we do this?"

"Let's start with the first item that you have a question about and work our way through the list, okay?"

Nodding Scott took a sip of his coffee and flipped to the start of the list. "Okay. So, what is *ageplay*?"

"That can mean several things, but generally it's when the sub acts younger than their age, such as an infant or toddler. The Dom then takes the role of caretaker."

"Okay, that one's a big no."

"Good, that one's a hard limit for me as well," Ross agreed.

It took them several hours to go through everything. The list that Ross had was extensive. Anytime he took on a new sub, he wanted to cover all the bases. After the disaster he'd had with Todd, he'd learned to be thorough. It was always best to understand all his sub's proclivities, not only the ones Ross might be interested in.

"Wow, I had no idea people would get off on some of that stuff," Scott said with a look of mild disgust.

"You shouldn't judge. Some people would find what you get off on equally distasteful."

"Yeah, I guess you're right," Scott agreed. "So, what about you? Do I get to know your kinks now?"

"Why don't we take a break and have some dinner first?"

Looking up at the clock Scott looked surprised. "Wow, I had no idea how late it was. Yeah, okay."

Ross decided to order pizza, keeping the evening casual. Once the pizza arrived, they continued their discussion in the kitchen. "We don't have to go through the list in detail again. I can tell you that your kinks and mine seem to align quite well. There are a few things you were hesitant about that are definite kinks of mine. We don't have to explore all of them at once. What I'd like to suggest now is to incorporate a few of them for the rest of your stay here this week. There are some that I think could help with your fears about us."

"Okay. At least this exercise has kept me so distracted I didn't have time to freak out today," Scott confessed.

"Good. I had a feeling that at least part of your anxiety came from getting stuck in your head. Thanks for confirming that."

"So, um ... what did you have in mind? For the rest of this week?"

"I'm glad you asked. You're too tense right now and I want to ease you into this. Will you come back to the study with me, please? We can discuss things in a little while."

Scott's frame stiffened in response, but he nodded. Ross could tell that his anxiety was ramping up again, and it was time to put a stop to it.

Entering the study, Ross first went to light the logs in the fireplace, before turning down the lights. Then he grabbed a pillow and placed it to the side of one of the wingback chairs. "I need to get you to relax. First, I want you to strip for me, please. Don't worry, we won't be doing anything sexual. This is to help you get into the right mindset. Nudity will increase your sense of vulnerability."

Scott's hands were trembling, but he obeyed. He hesitated when it came to his underwear. "All of it, please. You know I've already seen you naked. You have nothing to hide from me. Also, please fold everything and place it on the other chair."

Scott complied and then stood before Ross. He was a tight, shaking, bundle of nerves. "Has anyone ever told you how beautiful you are? I'm happy my soulmate is so gorgeous," Ross said as he caressed the side of Scott's face.

The praise had the effect that Ross had intended, and Scott's tension eased slightly, his eyes sliding closed as he leaned into Ross' touch. Ross turned away and sat down in the empty chair.

"Come here and kneel on this pillow next to me, facing the fireplace. Please."

Watching Scott sink to his knees nearly took his breath away. "Very good. Now, put your head in my lap and try to relax. Watch the fire."

Shuffling around to get comfortable, Scott slowly lowered his head. Ross then proceeded to run his hand gently through Scott's hair. Minute-by-minute, Scott slowly lost the tension in his body and relaxed against Ross' leg.

Drinking in Scott's submissive form and feeling him relax into his touch, instead of flinch away, made Ross' heart soar. *He's responding even better to this than I'd hoped. Please, Scott. Let me in. I promise to care for you like no one else ever could.*

After about a half-hour, Ross spoke, using a soft, gentle tone. "How do you feel now?"

It took a moment for Scott to respond. "Hmm. I feel … good. Relaxed. This is not at all what I was expecting."

"Excellent. I think we'll do this every evening after dinner this week. It's nice to have some quiet time to relax together. What do you think?"

"Yeah, I'd like that."

"Good. Now as for the rest of the week, let me tell you what I have in mind. You can tell me whether it sounds like something you might enjoy or not. I may still insist on one or two things you don't think you'll enjoy, but I want to focus on what you want first."

"How about letting me go back home and forget we ever met?" Scott joked.

Letting out an exasperated sigh, Ross rolled his eyes. "Very funny. I know you're still not happy with being my soulmate, but let's make the best of it, shall we?"

Scott took a deep breath and nodded. "You're right. I'm sorry. I shouldn't say things like that ... this isn't as bad as I thought it would be."

"First, let's discuss safewords. Instead of panicking and fleeing from me again, I want you to use a safeword if you can't immediately articulate when something is wrong. I find the stoplights system the easiest to remember. Red to stop anything we're currently doing or to let me know that you're feeling panicked. Yellow if you need us to slow down, pause, or you feel your anxiety building. Green if everything is good and we can proceed."

"Okay, that sounds easy enough to remember."

"What's your color right now?"

"Huh? Oh ... uh ... green, I guess."

"No anxiety right now?"

"Oh, well, yellowish-green? Not much anxiety. Maybe a tiny bit."

"Good boy. Thank you for being honest. Can you tell me what's causing the tiny bit of anxiety?"

Scott was silent for a long while and Ross continued running his fingers through his hair, trying to keep him calm.

"Okay, this is going to sound stupid, but ... I'm scared of letting myself like you. You seem like a great guy but..."

"but?"

"I've been repressing my attraction to guys for so long. I'm not entirely sure why. I know I'm sexually attracted to men, and yes I find you attractive," Scott admitted. "Yet, the idea of being with a guy always terrified me. Plus, since I'm also attracted to women, I always thought my soulmate would probably be a woman."

"Yet, here you are."

"Yeah. I told you it's stupid," Scott said with a shrug.

"It's not stupid. Same-sex soulmate pairs are very rare. If you found both sexes desirable, you had no reason to believe your soulmate would turn out to be male. I got lucky because I've never found women attractive, so somehow I knew my soulmate had to be male."

Scott relaxed against him again. "Talking like this is helping, but I still don't understand why I'm naked? Just to make me feel vulnerable?"

"I'm trying to build trust. By having you completely naked, and not doing anything sexual, I am hoping to gain your trust on a visceral level."

"Oh. Okay. That makes a lot of sense. But do you? Want to do sexual things with me?"

You have no idea.

"Oh yes, very much so. I told you that I find you beautiful. I loved holding you close to me when you were still unconscious, and I enjoyed running my hands all over that gorgeous body of yours," Ross confessed. "However, I will not rush into anything. We have some time now that the first stage of bonding has been completed, and you've recovered from your foolish attempt to break the bond."

"Yeah, sorry about that. I was so freaked out."

"It's alright. I'm beginning to understand."

"So, what else is on the itinerary?"

"I'd like to get you feeling comfortable with my touch, so I ask that you sleep in my bed with me. Underwear can be worn if you are uncomfortable sleeping naked."

"Okay, I think I can manage that."

"For breakfast tomorrow, I'd like you to kneel on a pillow like you are now and allow me to hand feed you."

"More trust building, I take it? Is that only for this week, or something you'd want to always do with me?"

"Why don't we try it for one meal and see how you feel about it?"

"Okay."

"Between meals, I'd like you to choose one non-sexual kink you'd like to explore with me, something like impact play, sensation play, or even some roleplaying."

"What ... what if I decide I want something sexual?"

"We'll discuss it and make sure you're ready for us to consummate our bond. We have several days yet before that has to happen, so no need to rush unless you're absolutely sure."

"If I'm never sure then you'll ... force me?"

"I am hoping it won't come to that, but if I'm going to be honest, then yes," Ross admitted. "For both of our sakes, I will, just the once. You know we need to consummate our bond. However, if you never want to have sex with me again, then I will respect that. I will be very disappointed, but I *will* respect it."

Scott slumped a bit. "Well, that's hardly fair. Once we're bonded, it's not like either of us will be able to have sex with anyone else," Scott said as he raised his left hand, looking at the darkened mark. "Once these marks are fully formed, there's no way to hide the fact we're bonded with a living soulmate."

"Let's cross that bridge when we get to it, okay?"

"Okay," Scott replied with a yawn.

Suddenly feeling sleepy himself, he ran his fingers through Scott's hair one last time before patting him on the back. "It's been a long day. Why don't we head to bed?"

"Yeah, that sounds good," Scott agreed.

Once they were prepared for bed, Ross was pleased to note that Scott chose to remain nude when slipping between the sheets next to him. Ross pulled him close and held him in his arms, which made Scott tense for a moment. "Shh, I only want to cuddle for a bit as we fall asleep. I promise. I really enjoyed falling asleep with you in my arms last night."

Scott relaxed again and shifted until he was comfortable. "Okay, g'night."

Staying awake as Scott slowly fell asleep in his arms, Ross was pleased with how the day had gone. Maybe there was hope for them after all.

SUBMISSION

Scott woke for the second day in the arms of his soulmate. He took a moment to think about how it made him feel. The instinct to panic and run wasn't there this time, which surprised him. Instead, he felt safe. *I wonder if Ross was right? Last night did go a long way toward building trust between us.* With no fear sparking his need to flee, he burrowed himself deeper into those arms. *I might as well get used to this. It does feel kind of nice.*

Emotions still warred within him. While Ross was slowly gaining his trust, he was also proving to be a caring and patient person. *More patient than I deserve after the stunt I pulled.* Scott still wasn't entirely sure why he'd been so terrified of *this*.

Since Ross was still sound asleep, Scott's mind wandered to the previous day. Finding out that Ross was into BDSM and preferred the dominant role hadn't even surprised Scott. He'd noticed Ross' dominance when they'd met at the burger joint, as well as his own instinct to submit to him. *Maybe that's part of why I freaked out? But that doesn't explain why I fled from him at the party.*

Still, talking about it with Ross and the little experiment they did had been more calming than he had expected. It had put Scott more at ease with everything. The little frisson of fear was still there in the back of his mind, but it wasn't as prominent as it had been. He had promised to give this a try, so he started thinking about the kinks they had discussed the day before and which ones most intrigued him.

The two that immediately came to mind were the ones classified under impact and sensation play. The idea of being bent over and having his ass spanked made his cock twitch. In the past, there had been a couple of ladies that had slapped Scott's behind during sex, and he recalled having enjoyed that. It was something he was willing to try with Ross. He also thought that the feel of melted candle wax being dripped onto his skin had sounded interesting.

As he mulled those and other possibilities over in his mind, Ross startled him. "What's going on in that head of yours?"

"Oh, hey. I didn't realize you were awake. I was ... um ... considering the two kinks you wanted me to pick out for today."

"You were? I'm proud of you for admitting that to me."

Heat flooded Scott's face, and he felt a happy ache in his chest at Ross' praise. "Oh, um, thanks," he replied. *Why does his approval make me feel like this?*

"So, do you know which kinks you want to try today?"

Scott nodded. "I was thinking maybe spanking and candle wax?" *Okay, and why does my dick love the idea of that spanking? Am I a masochist? Well, I am a novelist so ... very likely.* He chuckled internally at his own joke.

"Hmm, those are both excellent choices," Ross praised. "Will you come and shower with me?"

At the suggestion, the blood drained from Scott's face as his anxiety reared its head again and his entire body went taut. It was one thing to lie naked under blankets. In the shower, he'd feel so much more … exposed.

"Hey, it's okay. It's a shower. We get in, we wash, we get out. Nothing more, okay?"

Taking in a deep breath, Scott nodded. "Okay."

Come on, pull yourself together, Scott admonished himself. *It's not like I've never showered with someone before.* Getting up, he followed Ross into the bathroom, quickly using the facilities before joining Ross in the elaborate shower. "This thing is impressive," he said, trying to get out of his own head.

"Yeah. I love showers, so I wanted the fanciest one I could find."

"Fancy doesn't even do this thing justice," Scott joked. Enjoying the warm spray, Scott tried to get himself to relax. He watched Ross wash himself and couldn't help but admire the way his muscles moved beneath his skin. He almost didn't notice when Ross shoved the bottle of body wash into one hand, and a pouf into the other. "Hey, would you mind getting my back? I can never reach."

"Um … sure," Scott agreed

Scott put some more of the body wash on the pouf and lathered it up. Ross turned and Scott began to run the pouf along Ross' back, making several passes. The man had a beautiful back and a nice ass. Without even thinking, Scott was washing lower, until he was circling over the curves of Ross' behind.

"Mmm, that feels nice."

Embarrassed, Scott almost dropped the pouf. "Sorry, I didn't mean…"

Ross spun around and grabbed his wrist. "Hey, never apologize for touching me. You're my soulmate. I want you to touch me. I want … well, look down. You can see how much I want you."

Looking down, Scott's eyes went wide as he saw Ross' obvious arousal. His cock was slightly bigger than his own and beautifully shaped. Seeing how hard it was made his breath catch in his throat as he froze again. *How the hell is that ever going to fit inside me?*

Ross reached out and tilted his face up to look at him. "Hey, take a deep breath. Just because I want you, doesn't mean I'm going to pounce on you right now. I promised we'd take our time, and I meant it."

Scott nodded, and Ross caressed his cheek. The touch felt nice and Scott found himself leaning into it.

"Turn around, let me wash your back too, then we can get out of here, alright?"

Scott turned slowly and let Ross wash his back. It felt soothing and helped him relax again. A few minutes later, they were both out of the shower and drying off with big, fluffy towels.

"Are you okay remaining naked for me today?"

Wow, I wasn't expecting that. The anxiety of being so exposed warred with his very interested dick over the thought of that. Ross smirked when he looked down at Scott's twitching cock.

"Well at least part of you is on board with that idea," Ross teased.

Sighing in resignation, Scott agreed. "Alright, I'll try it, but what if I panic and feel the urge to put clothes on…?"

"Then tell me. We'll discuss it and if you still need to be dressed, you know where your clothes are," Ross reassured him.

"Okay."

"I'm going downstairs to make breakfast. You can join me now or come down when I call," Ross said as he slipped on a pair of jeans and a t-shirt.

"Can I help with something?"

"Sure, I'd like that. You can make the coffee."

Making their way down to the kitchen, Ross showed Scott how to use his fancy coffee machine, before going off to prepare breakfast. "I'm thinking pancakes, with a side of bacon. How does that sound?"

"That sounds perfect."

Soon there was a large plate piled with pancakes and bacon, along with mugs of steaming coffee, on the table. Ross went and grabbed a pillow from the window seat in the kitchen and plopped it next to his chair. Scott had almost forgotten about that part.

Ross sat and looked expectantly at him. Scott's heart hammered in his chest and he froze for a moment, before steeling himself and coming over to stand by the pillow. The food all looked good, and he was hungry. *I can do this. It wasn't so bad last night.*

Sinking to his knees on the pillow, Scott took several deep breaths to calm his nerves.

"Good boy. I'm proud of you for trying this with me. I'll feed you while I eat as well. Let me know when you're full, okay?"

"Okay," Scott agreed, taking some deep breaths, trying to still his mind from all the questions that kept swirling. *Is this what my life will be like from now on? Will he expect my complete submission and obedience?* His dick twitched again, and Scott wasn't sure what to make of that.

"Hey, eyes on me," Ross commanded. "Please stop getting lost in your head. I know you're used to your independence. I don't plan to take that away from you. This is about establishing trust between us, okay?"

Scott looked up at Ross and tried to focus on him. "Okay. I'll try."

"Focus on me and breakfast," Ross instructed as he held out a piece of bacon for him. "Open up."

Scott opened his mouth and accepted the food. He wasn't sure how he felt about being hand fed his food while on his knees at Ross' feet. It was oddly embarrassing and calming at the same time. "Try not to think about this too much. Be in the moment with me. We can analyze how you feel about it later."

"How did you—" Scott wanted to ask, when Ross slipped a piece of pancake into his mouth.

"Shh. Just eat."

Between bites and sips of coffee, Scott knelt and watched Ross enjoy his own breakfast as well. He tried being in the moment and not thinking about everything, instead focusing on Ross. How he carefully cut each piece of pancake, the way he chewed and swallowed. How he savored his coffee. Without even realizing it, soon breakfast was over, and Ross began clearing away the dishes.

"Did you get enough to eat? You never told me to stop feeding you."

"Yeah, I'm good. It was delicious and the perfect amount of food."

"That's good to know. Go ahead to the study and I'll meet you there."

Scott took his time on the way to the study. The house was spacious, but somehow it still felt cozy and comfortable. Once in the study, Scott decided to look through the bookshelves that lined the back wall of the room. Ross had some eclectic taste in literature. He saw everything from *Zen and the Art of Motorcycle Maintenance* to *2001: A Space Odyssey.*

"Do you like my collection?" Ross asked as he arrived.

"Yeah. Have you read all of these?"

"I have. I told you that I'm an avid reader," Ross reminded him as he made his way over to another bookshelf and pulled out a copy of Scott's most recently published novel. "In fact, I'd be honored if you'd autograph this for me."

Scott felt himself blush as Ross handed him the book and a pen from his desk. He opened it to the title page and signed his name. "I'm glad you liked it, but they aren't of the same caliber as what you've read," Scott said dismissively, gesturing to the small library before him.

"Hey, none of that. I really enjoyed how you described your world and characters. You write beautifully."

Scott shrugged, hoping Ross would change the subject.

Sighing, Ross ran his hand over Scott's autograph before placing the novel back on the shelf. "We'll have to work on that self-confidence of yours," Ross said. "So, about the rest of the day, I was thinking of giving you a tour of the estate and grounds first, and then doing the spanking scene before lunch. Afterward we can talk about the scene before doing the melted wax scene before dinner?"

A spike of nervous excitement ran up Scott's spine as Ross reminded him of the scenes he'd chosen to do today. Swallowing the lump in his throat he nodded. "That sounds ... okay."

"Hey, stay out of that head of yours," Ross reprimanded him. "I promise to ease you into all this and if it gets too much, you will have the power to stop everything. We'll discuss that more later. Go ahead and get dressed, since we'll be heading outside."

Visibly relaxing, Scott gratefully ran up to the bedroom. *For a minute there I thought he was going to make me go outside in the nude.*

Once Scott was dressed in a set of sweats and some sneakers, Ross showed him through the inside of the estate first. Starting downstairs, besides the kitchen, dining room, and study that he'd already seen, there was a living room with a large TV and another fireplace, a small theater room with a giant projection screen, a fully equipped gym, an indoor pool, and a recreation room with a bar, pool table, and another large TV with every kind of gaming console money could buy. Then heading upstairs, Ross took him to the wing opposite where Ross' master bedroom was located. "This wing belongs to the staff. Each one has their own suite, and there are a couple of unoccupied guest suites as well."

"Your staff actually lives here? Where are they?" Scott asked.

"I wanted us to have some privacy, so I gave them all some vacation time. They'll return in a few days to resume their duties."

The only room Ross didn't show him was near the master bedroom. "Don't worry about that one right now. We'll spend time in it later."

Smirking to himself, Scott imagined the room was a kinky sex dungeon. *With how much Ross talks about this BDSM stuff, I'd be surprised if he doesn't have a room like that.*

Next, they made their way outside, through a set of French doors in the dining room. Scott marveled at the size of the grounds. "The entire estate is about five-hundred acres," Ross explained. "The grounds you see here are about one hundred acres. The rest includes the surrounding woodland. I like my privacy."

"It's peaceful around here. I guess ... I'd be moving in here with you?"

"Are you okay with that? Moving into the estate with me?"

"Well, it does beat my ratty apartment," Scott admitted.

"We can discuss this more later, but if you need your own personal space, I can arrange something for you."

"Really? Even though you like bossing me around and stuff, you'd still let me do my own thing?"

Ross stopped walking and turned to Scott. "You're my soulmate, not my prisoner. I may enjoy being the dominant partner, but that doesn't mean I need to control everything about your life. Yes, if you need time to yourself in your own space, I'd be perfectly okay with that."

Feeling himself relax again, Scott couldn't help giving Ross a small smile. *Okay, maybe this whole soulmate thing won't be so bad after all.* "That's ... *really* good to hear. Thanks."

Sliding his hand into Scott's, Ross squeezed his hand. "However, if it turns out you want me to be in more control," Ross said with a sly grin. "I'd be okay with that, too."

Scott stared at Ross, trying to decide if he was joking. Ross gave an easy laugh and shrugged. "We'll cross that bridge if we come to it. Now, what do you say we make our way back inside and you let me warm that beautiful derriere of yours?"

Scott couldn't help the rush of blood that flooded his cheeks ... and his nether region. "Um, yeah, okay."

SPANKING

Ross was so pleased with how far Scott was progressing after only a day. It confirmed all his assumptions about him. The man *was* a natural submissive, who needed to be handled with care. Learning all of Scott's kinks also gave him a more complete picture of the man. He was pleased to learn that he and Scott shared an affinity for many of the same kinks.

Now he was leading Scott to the one room he hadn't included in the tour earlier. It was one of his favorite rooms of the house. The room was adjacent to the master suite but locked with a key. Ross had only two copies of the key. He always kept one key on him, and the other copy was kept in a safe in his study.

"Scott, I do not want you to panic when you see this room, okay? I'll walk you through everything you see here before we start our session, and there may be things we never use. Don't worry about any of that, okay?"

Scott nodded, but the tension returned to his frame. Ross grabbed his hand and held it. "Please, relax."

Then he pulled out his key and unlocked the door. He reached inside and flicked on the light switch before he led Scott inside. The audible gasp from Scott made Ross hold his hand a little tighter. "This is my playroom. I know it looks intimidating, but as I said, we may not use everything in here. If it's a hard limit on your list, it won't get used. Understood?"

"Yeah, okay."

"Good. Let me show you everything, and then we can proceed with the spanking, okay?"

"Okay."

"First, this room does have one rule, that will be enforced at all times. Subs must remove their clothing immediately upon entering this room and remain naked as long as they remain here. Strip for me, please."

Scott took some long, slow breaths before complying. Ross enjoyed watching the man reveal inch after inch of his beautiful body. He had to be patient, but he was looking forward to ravishing Scott when the time came.

Scott carefully folded his clothes as he removed them and placed them in a neat pile by the door. "Good boy. I'm happy you remembered to be neat with your clothes."

"Thanks."

"The furniture you see here serves similar purposes. Some I prefer for aesthetic reasons; others depend on mood or the nature of the scene I've planned," Ross explained as he led Scott over to the first piece. "This one, for example, is a spanking horse. You can straddle it like a horse or be bent over it. That one there is a spanking bench, which allows me to place more restraints and has more position options. The chair over there I like to use for over-the-knee spankings. That one on the wall is a St. Andrew's Cross, very useful if whipping is part of the scene. A sub can be both punished, fucked, or both on any one of these."

"Would I get a choice?"

"That depends on the scene and why we're using this room. Sometimes, yes, but not always. Today, you can choose."

"Okay."

"Over here," Ross said as he guided Scott over to the far wall. "Are all my various impact implements. As you can see, I have a variety of whips, switches, canes, crops, floggers, belts, straps, tawses, and paddles."

"Wow, there are so many kinds. What's that one?" Scott asked as he pointed to one of the more wicked looking implements.

"Ah, that's called a loopy johnny. It's primarily used for punishment, as it deals out a lot of pain without much effort. I do not recommend choosing that one for your first time."

"I'll take your word for it."

"Would you like to try a hand spanking today, or would you like a sampling of some of the implements as well?"

Scott was silent for a long time as he studied all the options hanging on the wall. "I ... don't know. What would you recommend?"

Ross smiled. He was hoping Scott would ask for his advice. "Okay, here is how I usually introduce a sub to impact play. I start with a light hand spanking, enough to warm up the buttocks. Then I give the sub three medium strikes from each type of implement. Each type comes in a variety of pain levels, so I choose the lowest level implement of each type. We could do that or do a longer hand spanking session."

After silently staring at the wall of implements for a few moments, Scott finally turned back to Ross with his decision. "I think I'll go with the hand spanking this time. The rest looks overwhelming right now."

"Wise choice," Ross said as he moved over to his spanking chair and sat down. "Come here and bend yourself over my knees then."

Ross tried not to smile when he noticed that Scott had begun to get aroused at the idea of the spanking, his cock already half-hard. Instead he focused on guiding the man over his spread legs and settled him as comfortably as possible.

Rubbing and kneading Scott's ass gently, Ross continued to reassure the skittish man bent over his knees. "Some people find spanking can be therapeutic. It releases endorphins into the brain and can uncover a well of emotion. Do not be ashamed if you feel the need to cry. That's a natural reaction. Also, remember your safewords if this becomes too intense for you."

"Red for stop, yellow for pause, green for I'm okay, right?"

"That's exactly right, my good boy."

Without further ado, Ross let the first smack land. It stung his hand and left a beautiful pink handprint on Scott's left ass cheek. He repeated the process on the right and then began to rain down strike after strike. Instead of counting, he was going for a combination of a particular shade of red and an emotional reaction from Scott.

He paused after about a half-dozen strikes to rub Scott's ass and check in with him. "How are you doing? What's your color?"

When Scott replied with *green*, he kept going. While he was spanking, he started asking other questions as well. It was when he began to ask about the other day that Scott began to sob. "Why did you need to get away from me so desperately that you were willing to risk your life?"

"I ... I don't know."

Smack. Smack. Smack.

"Why does the idea of bonding with a man terrify you so?"

"I'm not sure..."

Smack. Smack. Smack. Smack. Smack.

Suddenly all the tension in Scott's body seemed to drain away, and he went limp against Ross' legs as he began to sob.

"Scott? What's your color?"

"My dad ... it's because of my dad..." Scott admitted between sobs.

Ross immediately pulled Scott upright and pulled him into his lap, where Scott practically curled himself into his arms, sobbing uncontrollably. Stroking his hair, Ross let Scott cry himself out.

Once his sobbing eased, Scott sat up and looked at him. "Wow, that was intense."

"It can be," Ross said, wrapping his arms around Scott. "Are you ready to talk about it?"

"I suppose, yeah."

"Then *please* talk to me," Ross said as he caressed Scott's cheek and wiped away the tears.

"Okay, so my parents were soulmates ... not an unbonded couple. They were together for a few years before my mom got pregnant with me. I never got the whole story, but apparently my dad freaked when he found out and disappeared. He abandoned my mom and me. Her mark never faded, so we knew he was alive somewhere. It broke her heart ... I grew up hearing her cry herself to sleep every night. Because of her mark, she couldn't even find a new partner. No one would touch her. She kept going because of me, but once I was all grown up ... she died of a broken heart."

"That's why you're terrified of having a male soulmate? Are you afraid I'll do that to you?"

Scott nodded into his shoulder. "I don't want to end up like my mom."

Ross chuckled. "Do you see the irony here?"

Sitting up Scott looked at him and shook his head.

"You were afraid I was going to abandon you like your father did, so instead ... you very nearly abandoned me."

Looking stunned, Scott stammered. "Shit ... I'm ... damn, I'm so sorry. You're right. I'm *just* like my dad. I up and ran like the coward he was."

Ross took Scott's face into his hands. "Hey, you're not a coward. You're here now. I've forgiven you, and we'll work through this together, okay?"

Burrowing his face into Ross' shoulder, Scott nodded. "Yeah, okay."

"So, how'd you like the spanking?"

"Um ... not bad. It felt good at the beginning, but then all that emotional stuff came up. I think I still need to process this all first."

"That's fair. How about we clean ourselves up and get some lunch?"

"Yeah, that sounds good."

ACCEPTANCE

Scott took the last bite of lunch from Ross as he knelt at his feet again. They were eating in companionable silence, and he'd been thinking a lot about what happened with Ross earlier. It felt like a weight off his shoulders to admit to himself that he'd fled from Ross because of what had happened with his dad. However, it now weighed on his mind that he had almost done the same thing to Ross that his dad had done to his mom.

"Hey, a penny for your thoughts," Ross said as he scooted back from the table and looked down at him.

"I was thinking about how I almost did to you exactly what I was afraid of happening to me..."

"This is starting to eat you up, isn't it?"

Scott shrugged. "I can't help it."

"Do you feel like you need some way to earn redemption?"

Looking puzzled, Scott looked up at Ross. "How?"

"Well, I could punish you for running from me. If you take the punishment without complaint, then you're forgiven, and we start with a clean slate between us."

The thought of being punished to absolve him of his actions immediately made him sit up and take notice. "What kind of punishment?"

"From your limits list, you marked caning as a soft limit. I'm thinking I can have you bend over the spanking horse in the playroom and take five strikes from my cane. Does that sound fair?" Ross asked as he reached out and ran his fingers through Scott's hair gently.

His pulse quickened at the thought of that. On one hand he feared the pain of the strikes. On the other hand, the idea of taking the punishment felt cleansing. *Five strikes? I can handle that.* Scott nodded. "Yeah, more than fair."

"Good. Take the pillow up to the playroom. Kneel on it by the door and wait for me. I need to clean up the kitchen first."

"Okay."

Getting up, Scott grabbed the pillow and made his way to the playroom. On the way up, he realized he wasn't even feeling self-conscious about his nudity anymore. Ross hadn't tried to touch him sexually, and he was feeling completely relaxed around him now. He was starting to trust Ross, and that began to shift things in his mind. It was subtle, but he could feel some of his anxiety easing.

Putting the pillow down next to the playroom door, Scott sank to his knees and let his mind drift. He hadn't thought about his dad in years. All he had were photos that his mom had shown him. He wondered if the man was still alive somewhere. After his mom died, Scott had held on to the vague hope that maybe his dad would come and find him. His dad would have known when his soulmate had passed, because his own soulmark would have faded.

Next, Scott's mind drifted back to the night of the party when he first met Ross. Scott hadn't expected to meet his soulmate that night, much less someone like Ross. All he could remember was running away in a blind panic. He had merely reacted, there had been no conscious decision behind why he ran. That made him feel even more like shit. Maybe it was an ingrained instinct to flee from his soulmate, the same way his dad did? Could something like that be genetic?

Suddenly Ross stood in front of him, pulling him out of his reverie. "Are you ready?"

Swallowing thickly as his heart rate began to speed up, Scott nodded.

Ross opened the playroom door and led him inside. "Bend over the spanking horse. Do you want me to restrain you or can you hold position?"

Feeling the panic rise in his chest, Scott knew he'd need help. "Restrain me, please," he said as he bent over the horse.

"Thank you for being honest with me. What's your color?"

He was terrified, but he wanted absolution even more. He could do this. "Green."

Scott felt Ross slipping something around his ankles. "These are padded leather cuffs. They'll keep you secure without rubbing your skin raw."

Once his legs were secured, his wrists were next. Then Ross was rubbing over his previously spanked ass, kneading and massaging. "I'm going to give you a few swats with my hand first, to warm you up. Then you'll take five strikes from the cane."

Without further ado, Ross' hand rained down swift smacks across his ass. A tingle and warmth began to build as the smacks stopped. "Your ass looks good all warm and pink like this," Ross praised. "I do hope you let me do this in the future."

Then Ross made his way toward his wall of implements. Scott watched as he picked through his collection of canes. Settling on one, he made his way back to Scott. "After each strike, I would like you to count and apologize."

"Okay," Scott acknowledged.

The cane tapped his ass three times before Scott heard the cane whipping through the air, just before it cracked against his skin, bringing with it a bright stripe of pain. Scott yelped and took a breath before making the count.

"One. I'm sorry."

Crack.

"Ow! Two. I'm sorry!"

Crack.

"Three ... Sorry. So sorry!"

Crack.

"Fu ... four. I'm sorry. I'm sorry!"

Crack.

"F ... f ... five. Sorry! I shouldn't have run from you. I'm so sorry!"

Tears were streaming down his face, but it was over. Ross was unfastening the cuffs and pulling him onto his feet and wrapping his arms around him. "You took your punishment so well. I'm very proud of you. You're forgiven."

"Th ... thank you. I really am so sorry I ran from you." Scott sobbed. He felt a mix of regret and relief while he clung to Ross.

"Let me put everything away and then I'll put some ointment on your ass. I didn't strike to break skin, but there's no need for it to hurt more than necessary."

A few moments later, Scott was lying face down on the bed in the master suite while Ross was rubbing ointment over his welts.

"We're going to skip the melted wax play," Ross declared. "I think you've been through enough today. How do you feel about me ordering Chinese food and playing video games this evening?"

"That sounds like fun," Scott said, enjoying the gentle touches from Ross as he continued to work the ointment into his abused skin.

"Throw some sweats on, if you want. I'll go downstairs and order. Is there any kind of Chinese food you don't like?" Ross asked as he gave one last dab of ointment on a welt before getting up.

"Nah, it's all good."

* * *

After Ross left to call in the delivery order, Scott thought about everything that had happened. He felt less weighed down, as if his soul itself felt lighter. *It's amazing that something as simple as being punished and forgiven could do that. Ross was right, that did make me feel better.*

Scott headed into the master bath and looked at his ass in the large mirror. It was pink, and the welts were a deep red. It felt hot to the touch as he ran his hands over both throbbing globes. *It hurts, but it feels so good at the same time. I had no idea I was so kinky.*

After admiring his rear for another moment, he went to the closet to grab some sweats. As he began dressing, Scott's mind flitted back to his childhood and all the times he'd walked in on his mother weeping as she caressed her soulmark. The memory still made his heart clench with sadness.

He had tried to do everything he could to bring his mother happiness, but the hole his father had left in her heart seemed irreparable. Scott always felt that it had been his fault. Knowing that his father had run away after discovering his soulmate was pregnant, had always weighed heavily on him. However, his mother had never blamed him. She had always done her best to reassure him that it had nothing to do with her becoming pregnant.

Yet, why else had the man run off? Did he also suffer from bouts of intense panic? A wave of guilt knotted in his stomach. *I can't believe I almost did that to Ross. I'm such a coward. I don't deserve him...*

Scott hadn't realized he had curled up on the floor, shaking and on the verge of tears until Ross was hauling him up onto the bed and into his arms. He shamelessly clung to Ross, heaving sobs into his shoulder. "It's okay, Scott. I have you. I'm sorry, I shouldn't have left you alone after a punishment like that."

The emotions crashed over him in waves as Scott wept. "I'm sorry for being such a loser, Ross. You deserve ... you shouldn't be burdened with a broken soulmate like me."

Ross pulled him away from his shoulder and forced him to look into his eyes. "Scott Hansen, you will not disparage yourself. We're soulmates and that means we're perfect for each other. You are not a burden. I needed someone in my life that I could take care of, and here you are. Do not ever think you're not good enough for me."

"But—" Scott was about to argue when he found himself hauled over Ross' knees. His sweatpants were swiftly pulled down, and he howled as Ross laid several powerful spanks across his already sore ass cheeks.

A moment later, his sweats were back in place and he was wincing as Ross sat him back up again.

"Let's try this again," Ross said sternly. "You are my soulmate, and you are exactly what I need in my life, and I am exactly what you need. Do not second guess fate. Do I make myself clear?"

"Yes, Sir," Scott said even as he winced at the pain coming from his freshly spanked ass.

Ross smiled at him. "That's better. Thank you for being so polite. Now, how about that Chinese food?"

* * *

A few hours later and Scott was laughing as he beat Ross at Mario Kart. *Again.*

"That is unreal. How can you be this good at a game you haven't played since you were a kid?" Ross asked with a laugh.

"Natural talent, I guess?" Scott teased.

After everything that had happened, Scott felt more at ease now than he had in a long time. Ross was nothing like he'd expected to find in a partner, but he began to see why they were born to be soulmates.

Ross had put down his controller and was studying him. Suddenly the atmosphere changed, and Scott's breathing sped up as Ross took his controller out of his hands and leaned in closer. "Scott..."

Feeling an almost magnetic force pulling him closer, Scott closed the gap between them as their lips met. Ross' lips were warm and soft, but he didn't kiss anything like the ladies Scott was used to. All of Ross' understated dominance came to the fore as he took control of the kiss, slipping his hand around the back of Scott's neck, pulling him even closer. Scott groaned and parted his lips as Ross' tongue flicked out, swiping across his bottom lip before delving deeper.

He could practically feel their bond growing stronger as they explored each other's mouths and Ross gently gripped his hair to control the angle of his head. When they parted, they were both panting. Scott flicked his eyes up to meet Ross' gaze. "Wow."

"Yeah. Was that okay?"

"More than okay," Scott murmured before diving in for another round. The video games forgotten, Scott let himself be kissed into a blissful stupor.

When they parted again, Ross slipped his hand around to cup Scott's face. "You're amazing, Scott. You've come a long way in the short time we've been together."

Staring into Ross' gorgeous green eyes, Scott swallowed thickly, and leaned into Ross' touch. "You're pretty amazing yourself. I'm really glad you found me and I'm glad that stupid stunt I pulled didn't permanently break our bond."

"I'm glad, too. For both our sakes," Ross said, giving Scott another brief kiss. "I'm happy that you're taking to all this so well."

Smiling at Ross, Scott gave a small shrug. "You really know what you're doing. Everything you've suggested has helped put me at ease."

"That's what I was hoping for. You've really exceeded my expectations," Ross praised.

"So, what's the plan for tomorrow?" Scott asked.

"You've come a lot farther today than I expected. Tomorrow, I'd like to take it easy. Let's spend time together and talk about everything that happened today. Maybe go for a hike? I've got some beautiful trails on my property. I'd also love to take you out for a romantic dinner, if you're up for that?"

"Yeah, that all sounds great ... but..."

"But...?"

"Well, how soon do we need to do this consummation thing?"

"Our marks aren't causing problems yet, but I suspect they'll start irritating us again by the end of the week."

"So, I still have a few days to get used to all this? Okay, that's cool. I have more questions, but they can wait until tomorrow."

"Okay, baby. I'll answer anything you ask."

"Baby? Really?" Scott scoffed playfully.

"Okay, I'll work on the pet name."

That night, Scott snuggled in Ross' arms, with one fleeting thought that ran through his mind as he drifted off to sleep. *I really could get used to this...*

BONDING

Ross smiled when he slowly woke with Scott in his arms. For a change he found himself awake first, so he savored the moment, snuggling closer to his soulmate.

Yesterday had gone far better than he could have dreamed. Scott responded to everything perfectly. After how eagerly Scott returned his kiss last night, he hoped Scott was warming up to him. Regardless, he and Scott would have to consummate their bond soon, and Ross was looking forward to ravishing this beautiful man.

Getting Scott to understand the source of his fear had been a big breakthrough. He wondered what had become of Scott's father. Ross decided he should try to find out if the man was even still alive. It would give Scott the closure he clearly never had.

Despite the short time he'd known Scott, he was completely smitten by him. There was something about him that brought out Ross' protective side. Despite his need to be the dominant partner, he already knew he was going to spoil Scott rotten.

Having Scott in his arms felt wonderful and made his heart soar with happiness. Ross couldn't hold back any longer, and he began to trail kisses along the line of Scott's neck. He kissed slowly down toward his shoulder until Scott began to stir in his arms.

"Mmm. That's a nice way to wake up."

"Good morning. I'm glad to hear it. How are you feeling this morning?"

Scott turned and faced him. "A lot better, about everything. Also, a little sore. I think I'm going to avoid doing anything that's going to get me *punished* like that again."

"Good. I don't enjoy punishing my subs. I prefer to bring them pleasure. All I want to do is make you happy, Scott."

"I'm starting to see that. I'm so sorry I fucked up."

"Stop that. You took your punishment and you're forgiven. Put that behind you now, okay?"

"Yeah, I know. Bear with me while I get used to the new normal. I'm used to obsessing over my mistakes," Scott confessed.

"I figured. I'll get you out of that habit. It's not healthy."

"Yes, *daddy*," Scott teased.

"Okay, no. You vetoed baby. I'm going to veto daddy," Ross said with a laugh. "How do you feel about ... *sweetheart*?"

"For you or me?" Scott asked.

"As an endearment I can call you?"

"Well ... try it first?"

"Okay, *sweetheart*. How does that sound?"

Ross felt a shiver run through Scott and he smiled at him with a little nod. "Okay, I like that one. How about for you?"

Ross sat up a bit and looked down at Scott. "We haven't really discussed this yet, since I've been easing you into everything. Most of the time, I'm fine with being called by my name.

However, if we continue doing scenes together like we did yesterday, I prefer being addressed as *Sir*."

"What if I decide I don't want to do any more scenes with you?" Scott asked as he sat up as well.

Ross frowned. "Well, I'd respect that ... but I can't say I wouldn't be disappointed. So, you didn't enjoy anything we did yesterday?"

Scott laughed. "Don't worry. I enjoyed everything more than I expected, but I had to ask. I'm not sure if I'm ready to agree to doing it all the time or whatever."

"I wouldn't insist on it being all the time, unless it turned out that's what's best for our dynamic," Ross said. "Even then, we'll have to discuss it in greater detail and find the right balance that works for both of us. Besides, I still want to hang out and play video games and other fun things on occasion too."

"Okay, that's reassuring. Last night was a lot of fun. I haven't played video games in ages."

"It's more fun with someone else to play with," Ross winked as he disentangled himself and got up. "Join me in the shower?"

Scott looked at Ross, eyes flicking down to his obvious erection and blushed.

"Now don't tell me you never get morning wood?" Ross teased.

Scott laughed. "That's not why I'm blushing ... um or rather..." He pushed away the blankets to reveal his own arousal.

"Am I starting to have an effect on you, sweetheart?" Ross asked as he crawled over the bed toward Scott.

"Um ... *maybe?*"

Ross leaned down and captured Scott's mouth in a searing kiss. After breaking away, Ross saw there was still a hint of uncertainty in Scott's eyes. "Hey, don't worry, I told you I'm not going to rush this. I'm happy you're starting to relax around me."

Ross crawled off the bed and made his way into the bathroom. Slowly Scott's walls were coming down, but Ross knew he still had to take his time. Smiling to himself, he realized that by being forced to take things slow with his soulmate, brought out the protective Dom in him. Maybe this was how their dynamic was meant to develop since he was very quickly falling for Scott. More quickly than if he and Scott had made passionate love the first night they met, like so many other soulmates did.

When Scott made his way into the bathroom, Ross smiled warmly at him. They prepared for their day much as they had the morning before, only this time Scott was able to get fully dressed. Today they both wore jeans and hoodies, and Ross suggested comfortable shoes if they were going to go for a hike later.

After breakfast, Ross prepared a picnic lunch and packed it into a backpack, before leading Scott outside, toward his favorite trail. At first, they walked in companionable silence, enjoying the crisp autumn air.

Scott was the first to speak. "So, um ... about yesterday?"

"Yeah? You can say or ask me anything," Ross replied.

"When you brought up that I had tried to run, like my dad did? That ... that got to me. I haven't thought about him in so long. Do you think he's still alive somewhere?"

"It's possible. Would you like me to help you find out?"

"Yeah, I think so. I've always thought about it, but I wouldn't even know how to start."

"I know some guys. Do you know his name and birthdate at least?"

"Oh, yeah. Back at my place I've got all the paperwork that my mom kept. It's got their marriage certificate and everything."

"Perfect. If he is still alive, do you want to meet him or know the truth before you decide?"

"I'm not sure. I do have a lot of questions for him if I ever get the chance, but ... I don't want to get my hopes up before I know if he's still around or not."

"Okay. Let's find out if he's still among the living first, and then you can decide."

"Thanks," Scott replied as he looked around and changed the subject. "Your estate is gorgeous. Did you develop it?"

"Some of it, yes. I worked with a team to design the house and grounds. I knew I wanted to keep a large portion undeveloped as well. I enjoy the peace and quiet, and it gives me a measure of privacy."

"Do you have any other buildings on the property?"

"Only what you've seen, why?"

"Oh, nothing. I was only thinking a little cabin in these woods might make for a nice retreat sometimes."

"I like how you think," Ross praised, reaching out and slipping Scott's hand into his. "It would be especially nice for a writer who might need to get away from his soulmate whenever he wanted to focus on his writing ... *right*?"

Scott allowed his hand to be held as he ducked his head and nodded. "Yeah. You have me all figured out already, don't you?"

"No need to be embarrassed, I think it's a great idea. Tell me what you want, and I'll make sure it meets all your needs."

"Just like that?"

"Yeah, just like that. Nothing's too good for my soulmate."

Scott paused and tightened his grip on Ross' hand, pulling him closer. "You're going to spoil me, aren't you?"

Ross was pleasantly surprised by Scott's new forthrightness. Smiling, he leaned in even closer. "You have no idea."

Scott wrapped his arms around Ross and kissed him before leaning their foreheads together. "Thanks for putting up with me. I'm still really sorry for everything."

Ross blinked back the sting of emotion in his eyes, while reaching up and caressing Scott's face. "You've been forgiven for that, remember? Unless you want me to bend you over the next fallen log and warm your ass some more?"

Laughing, Scott shook his head. "No, my ass has been reminding me of that punishment from yesterday with every step. It's only ... I'm starting to think you're my ideal partner, and I nearly ruined it for both of us."

"Well, you can spend the rest of your life making it up to me, okay?"

Scott laughed again. "Yeah, okay."

* * *

Later that day found Scott and Ross relaxing in front of the fireplace in the study, each occupying a wingback chair. "We need to talk about how we should proceed," Ross said. "We've had a bit of a rough start, and I know you're not looking forward to all the publicity that will come from it, but after we consummate our bond, we won't be able to keep it a secret."

"Yeah, I know. We'll need to register our bonding and then it'll be public knowledge. I guess ... well at least my publisher will be pleased. It'll help sell more books."

Ross chuckled. "That it will. We need to figure out how we want to announce it. If it comes out that it took us so long to consummate, you know there'll be an inquiry."

Scott nodded. "Yeah ... fuck. It's all my fault, but we'll both get blamed, won't we?"

"They'll know we both attended the same party, so we can't lie about that. They don't know when either of us arrived or left though, so we could say we missed each other."

"Yeah, but then how'd we meet? We don't move in the same circles."

"You're right. We need our story to have an element of truth in it, without looking like there was an outright rejection."

"How about this? I drank too much, got sick, and passed out. You brought me home and nursed me back to health and we decided to take time to get to know each other better before ... everything."

"I like it. That's close enough to what actually happened. We can fudge the days a bit, in between."

"So, what can I expect? I still remember that one same-sex couple back when I was a kid. Will we have to do all that, too?"

"In order to get ahead of the situation, we should hold a press conference. I can get one scheduled immediately after we register. Afterward, we'll be expected to go on a press tour as well, making the rounds at all the talk shows and such. Once that's over with, things should quiet down."

Ross noticed that Scott's hands had a white-knuckle grip on the arms of his chair. Getting up, he went over and took Scott's hand in his, pulling him up. "Hey, I'll be with you the entire time. I can do most of the talking if you prefer."

Scott took a deep breath. "Yeah, okay. So ... do you still want to wait to consummate until the end of the week?"

"That's up to you. You know how much I want you ... I'll happily take you any time," Ross growled. "We'll only have to be prepared for the whirlwind that will follow once we do."

"Yeah, that's what I'm most afraid of now."

"Then we wait a few more days," Ross said with a shrug.

"Isn't it driving you crazy? I'm sorry I'm making you wait so long," Scott apologized.

"On some level it is, but it's been enjoyable to take the time to get to know you. I think this time together will bring us closer and hopefully make the whole media circus more tolerable."

"Yeah, having you at my side through all that will help. You're really good at calming my nerves."

"Good, I'm glad you think so. I'll do my best to make it as painless of a process as I can. Thankfully, I have some connections and we can take my private jet."

Scott's eyes widened before shaking his head. "Why am I even surprised you have a private jet? How much are you worth, anyway?"

"Well, that depends on market fluctuations," Ross teased. "Honestly, I'd have to look. I'm not entirely sure."

"Alright, Mr. Rich Guy, didn't you promise to take me out to dinner?"

"Hmm, I'd love to, but aren't I supposed to be nursing you back to health?"

"Oh, yeah."

He could see Scott deflate a little at the reminder. "I know I promised to take you out tonight, but now I don't think it's wise. I'll wine and dine you properly the night we consummate the bond. Okay?"

"Yeah, that sounds nice," Scott said, perking up.

Ross smiled. He was going to give Scott a romantic evening he'd never forget.

CONSUMMATION

Scott kept fidgeting with his tie, as his nerves started to get the better of him again. This was the first time he and Ross were going to dine out together in public since Ross had rescued him from his own stupidity. Since then Ross had done a lot to assuage his fears, and Scott was genuinely enjoying the man's company. In fact, he could see himself falling for Ross, and they had grown closer in the past week. Scott was blown away by how much affection Ross already held for him.

"Hey sweetheart," Ross said. "The limo is here. Are you alright?"

"Yeah. I'm a little nervous, I guess."

"You look so handsome, like the first night I saw you."

Scott felt heat creep into his cheeks.

Ross stepped closer and caressed his face. "Have I told you that you look adorable when you blush?"

Scott shook his head.

"Well, you do," Ross said, taking his hand and leading him out of the bedroom. "Now let's go. We can't be late for our reservation."

They made their way downstairs and out of the main entrance, where a limo was waiting for them. Scott had never ridden in one before and he was amazed at the interior. As they settled in, Ross opened a door on a minibar and began to pour them both a drink. He handed Scott a glass and raised his. "Tonight is going to be a night of firsts, and a night for celebration. To us."

They clinked as Scott agreed. "To us."

As he sipped on his drink, Scott stared out of the window for a while. He wondered where they were dining. Ross wouldn't tell him, wanting it to be a surprise. Sneaking a peek at his soulmate, he saw that Ross was watching him, which made Scott blush again.

"Am I really worth staring at?"

"Of course. Don't you know how handsome you are?"

Scott shrugged. "I suppose. I always found plenty of ladies to take to bed, so I figured I must be decent looking."

"You're far more than *decent looking*. You're absolutely gorgeous," Ross purred.

"Well, you're easy on the eyes too," Scott admitted.

"Flattery will get you everywhere, sweetheart," Ross said with a wink. "Especially tonight."

Rolling his eyes, Scott went back to staring out of the window, but he couldn't help the smirk that crossed his lips. He realized they were heading into the city, and soon they were wending their way through downtown. The limo stopped at an unexpected location, outside of an upscale hotel. As the driver opened the door for them to exit, Ross took Scott's hand and began to lead him inside. "Is this one of your properties?"

"Yes, and the top five-star hotel in the city," Ross beamed with pride.

They entered the lobby, and it was clear they were expected. Several staff members were there to greet Ross and ushered them to a private elevator that required a key. "I maintain a private suite. When I'm working in the downtown office, I sometimes have very late nights and it's easier for me to crash here, than make it all the way back to the estate," Ross explained.

They rode up the elevator in silence. Scott wasn't sure what to expect since he thought they were going to some fancy restaurant. When the elevator stopped, and the doors opened, Scott was immediately blown away.

Ross had a wide grin on his face as he led Scott out of the elevator and into the penthouse suite. The entire space was lit with a myriad of fairy lights. The effect was magical.

Taking his hand, Ross guided him toward a table set for two, placed by the wall of floor-to-ceiling windows that overlooked the cityscape below. There was a man dressed as a waiter standing by to pull the chairs out for them, assisting Scott first.

Until now Scott had been speechless. As he sat and looked around and then back at Ross, all he could manage was, "Wow."

"You like it?"

"It's amazing. I thought you were taking me to some upscale restaurant in the city. I never expected ... this."

"Well, you're going to be thrust into the public eye tomorrow, so I figured you'd appreciate having dinner in a more private setting tonight."

"That's so considerate. I hadn't even thought of that, but thanks."

"Anything for you, sweetheart."

The adoring look Ross was giving him had his heart stuttering in his chest. For the thousandth time, he felt foolish for having tried to run away from this fate. "You're an amazing man, Ross. I'm damned lucky that you're my soulmate."

"That makes two of us," Ross said with a warm smile as he gestured for the waiter who came over and poured them each a glass of wine. "We're ready for the first course."

Ross had arranged for a full six-course meal and Scott was both amazed and slightly overwhelmed by everything. He was relieved when dessert was served. "This dinner has been amazing. I never knew you could have so many courses in one meal."

Chuckling, Ross nodded. "I wasn't raised on this kind of food, but I enjoy it for special occasions. I think tonight definitely counts, don't you?"

Feeling the heat rise in his cheeks, thinking of what would come next, Scott nodded. "Yeah, it is."

"Still nervous?"

"A little," Scott admitted. "I … I've never been with a guy before."

"I'll make sure your first time is amazing, sweetheart," Ross said as he stood up and crossed the room. Scott rose as well, and the waiter immediately cleared away the dishes and some other staff removed the table and chairs before leaving the two of them alone.

Pouring two drinks from a decanter that was set up on a small table, Ross handed one to Scott, before taking his hand and leading him into a sunken living room with a blazing fireplace in the center.

"I'm going to take my time seducing you, sweetheart. We have all night and I'm going to make sure we do this right."

Nodding, Scott watched as Ross loosened his tie and unbuttoned the top button of his shirt. Scott felt his pulse quicken, and he took a swallow of his drink. *Brandy,* his mind supplied.

Following suit, Scott also undid his tie before allowing Ross to pull him down onto the couch next to him. They both took another sip before setting their glasses aside and Scott turned to look at Ross. The five o'clock shadow that had grown in since the man had shaved this morning outlined his strong jawline, and his green eyes sparkled in the firelight.

"Penny for your thoughts," Ross said as he reached out and gently ran his fingers over Scott's face and slid his hand around his neck.

"I was admiring the view," Scott admitted, allowing himself to get pulled closer.

Ross' hand cradled the back of Scott's head as he closed the distance between them, capturing Scott's mouth. Ross' rough stubble contrasted with the soft plush of his lips and the warm slide of his tongue. The taste of brandy was there, along with Ross' own heady scent.

Scott lost himself in the kiss as the blood began to rush south. His own hands traveled up and wrapped around Ross, needing to feel the man in his arms. Time seemed to stand still as Ross ravished his mouth, and he almost yelped when he felt Ross' other hand began to stroke his arousal through his slacks.

"You're already hard for me, sweetheart," Ross observed, his voice rough with his own arousal.

His tongue felt thick in his mouth, swallowing hard Scott merely nodded.

"Do you want me as much as I want you? I've wanted to push you against a wall and fuck you so hard all week."

His heart stuttered at those words, said with such raw passion. "Yeah, I'm ready."

"Let's take this to the bedroom," Ross suggested, kissing him hard one more time before standing and taking his hand, leading him to a set of stairs Scott hadn't noticed before. Once upstairs, he saw that the bedroom was a loft that overlooked the same cityscape they had dined in front of. He realized they were about to make love in front of that amazing view, and the thought made Scott feel shy again.

Ross gently grabbed his chin. "Hey, eyes on me. Don't worry, no one can see us. I promise."

Nodding, Scott tried to ignore the view and focus on Ross, but it was hard. His anxiety came flooding back all at once and he froze. *All those people, they're out there. I can feel all those eyes staring ... judging...*

"Hey, do you need me to be Ross right now, or do you need me to be your Sir?" Ross asked. "Tell me what you need, sweetheart."

"I ... I don't know what I need. A moment ago, all I wanted was you, but now ... I'm terrified again."

"What's terrifying you?"

"All those eyes ... out there. Maybe they can't see, but it feels like they're all watching us right now. Judging us. *Judging me.*"

"Thank you for admitting that, sweetheart. I think you need me to be your Sir right now. Will you consent to my dominance of you?"

Scott looked at Ross and saw the feral lust reflected in his eyes. Without even thinking, he simply slipped to his knees. "Yes, Sir. I consent."

"Good boy," Ross praised. "Do you remember the safewords?"

Scott nodded.

"Use your words."

"Yes, Sir. Red for stop, yellow for pause, green for everything is good."

"What's your color right now?"

"Yellow, Sir."

"Why is your color yellow? Talk to me, sweetheart."

"I'm ... panicking, Sir."

"Alright, I'll try to fix that, but I need for you to strip first. Can you do that for me, sweetheart?"

Scott nodded and complied with the command, getting back on his feet. His hands shook as he took off his suit jacket and began to unbutton his shirt. Ross came toward him and closed a hand over Scott's, stilling them. "Here, let me help."

Moments later and Scott was completely bare, while Ross remained clothed, except for his suit jacket. Ross sat down on the end of the bed. "Would you like me to take your focus away from the windows?"

"Yes, Sir."

"How do you feel about me warming your ass? Not as a punishment but to help focus your mind?"

The previous impact play they had done had helped to ground and center him in a way that nothing else ever had, and the idea made his cock harden further. *Fuck, why does this always turn me on?* "That sounds like a good idea, Sir."

"Then go into the bathroom over there," Ross pointed at a door. "Grab the hairbrush on the counter and give it to me."

A shiver of excitement ran through him at the picture that painted in his head. "Yes, Sir."

Scott made his way into the bathroom, seeing the wooden hairbrush that sat on the counter. It looked like it had never been used. Ross must have made sure to have it on hand in case Scott's bottom needed warming. Grabbing it, he noted the weight of it and realized this was going to sting when applied to his ass. He turned off the light and hurried back to Ross.

"Here you go, Sir."

"Good boy. Come here and bend over my lap. Let's see if I can't get you out of your head."

Bending himself over Ross' lap, he was positioned until his ass was presented. Ross spread his knees to give Scott more stability and to leave Scott's erection dangling free.

Ross' hand was warm as it caressed and kneaded his butt cheeks. "Take some deep breaths, sweetheart. Focus on my touch."

Scott focused on Ross' hands, the one at the back of his neck, holding him down, and the other caressing his ass. He took several deep breaths, and he felt the tension slowly leave his body.

"What's your color now?"

"Getting greener, Sir."

"Good boy. I'll warm your ass to a nice shade of pink. Shall we begin?"

A shiver ran through him at the words and he had to take another breath before responding.

"Yes, Sir."

The hand on his ass lifted away and Scott could hear him picking up the brush. The first swat was light but still made him yelp in surprise. Ross slowly built up the strength and speed as he continuously smacked his ass. The smacks stung but left behind a tingle that became a spreading warmth. The warmth layered upon itself and began to increase in intensity, making Scott squirm under the continued assault.

Every swat seemed to go directly to his dick. Scott was now leaking pre-come all over the floor and his entire world narrowed down to the heat in his ass. He was surprised at how close he was to coming.

The smacks stopped, leaving his ass throbbing and hot. "Are you still worried about all those non-existent eyes?"

"No, Sir."

Ross' hand reached down and stroked Scott's rock-hard cock a couple of times, making him moan. "You are so hard for me. Are you ready now, sweetheart?"

"Yes, Sir. *Please?*"

"That's what I was hoping to hear," Ross said as he gave Scott a couple of firm strokes, bringing him right up to the edge.

Ross repositioned him so he was sitting in his lap, and Scott curled into his embrace. "Hey, how do you feel?"

"That was amazing. You got me out of my head, but I was surprised at how much that aroused me."

"Do you think you could have come if I had continued?"

"Maybe? I think I might have, Sir."

"Hmm, we may have to explore that further on another day," Ross said with a chuckle. "Do you still need me to be your Sir? I can be, but I think I'd rather be your soulmate right now."

"I'm ready for my soulmate. Thanks, Ross."

"Get up on the bed then, sweetheart," Ross said as he stood and began undressing. "How's your ass feel?"

"Tender, but I ... kind of like it."

"Good, because I liked warming your ass. It's a beautiful shade of pink and it looks good on you," Ross admitted as he grabbed a bottle of lube and dropped it onto the bed next to Scott. "Now, I am going to drive you crazy with desire before I finally take you and make you mine forever."

Scott's entire body shuddered at those words. "Fuck, I don't think I've ever been this turned on before ... and you want to turn me on even more?"

"Oh, yes, much more. I want you begging for me." Ross purred as he leaned down and captured Scott's lips. After kissing him breathless, Ross worshiped every inch of Scott's body, kissing, licking, and exploring. No partner had ever paid this much attention to him before. Scott was getting drunk from pure pleasure.

When Ross finally reached down and began playing with Scott's hole, he was so relaxed he almost didn't notice the intrusion. He did take notice when Ross began sliding his finger in and out, stroking his prostate with every inward thrust.

"Fuck, that feels good," Scott groaned as he arched his hips.

"Mmm, I'm glad it does, sweetheart. I'd like to start doing this a lot more often after tonight."

"If it always feels this good, then you have a deal."

"I must be doing something wrong. You're far too lucid," Ross teased, before ducking down and taking Scott's cock in his mouth, causing Scott's first cry of ecstasy.

The warm, wet heat of Ross' mouth, in conjunction with a second finger sliding into his ass made Scott lose his coherence as he arched farther off the bed. Ross continued to lavish his attention on Scott's cock while working his hole open with his fingers. He never knew being filled up like this would feel so fantastic. "Please, Ross. *Please*, I need more..."

"That's more like it," Ross praised, sliding his fingers out and leaving Scott feeling strangely empty. "With you begging like that, I don't think I can wait any longer."

"Yes, please," Scott continued to beg. "I feel so empty ... *please*."

"Do you need me to fill up that tight hole of yours?" Ross purred into his ear.

"Yes, please. I need you inside me. *Please*."

Ross moved between Scott's legs, using his hands to spread his thighs wide. Scott watched as Ross slicked up his hard cock before guiding himself into Scott's well-prepared hole. As the head breached him for the first time, Scott arched his hips up. He winced at the slight burn as his muscles tried to accommodate the stretch around Ross' cock. Immediately Ross slowed, rocking in and out gently until Scott felt the burn ease.

Once his muscles relaxed around Ross, Scott eagerly angled his hips to take the cock deeper. "That's it, sweetheart, open up for me. Let me into that sweet hole of yours."

When Ross was fully inside of him, Scott's mark began to tingle.

"Do you feel that? Our bond is starting to form..." Ross said as he leaned down and kissed Scott deeply, giving him time to adjust before he started to move. "You're so hot and tight for me sweetheart, so perfect ... and all *mine*."

Scott could barely register Ross' words as he was consumed by ecstasy. The pure pleasure he felt as Ross thrust into him over and over was overwhelming. Whenever Ross grazed his prostate on a thrust, Scott would cry out, his own cock throbbing and leaking.

His mark began to pulse in time with Ross' thrusts and Scott arched his back, his hips meeting Ross'. It was as if a missing part of him had found its way home and Scott was unwilling to let it go. He needed to keep Ross inside of him.

Feeling a desperate need to come, Scott slid his hand down toward his cock, but Ross grabbed it and pushed it over his head. "Oh, no sweetheart, not yet."

He cried out in frustration when Ross grabbed his other hand and held them both above his head, entwining their fingers. Instead Scott changed the angle of his hips until he felt Ross hit that spot of blinding pleasure inside of him again and again. Ross began thrusting harder, faster, going deeper at the new angle.

It was not enough and too much at the same time, and Scott began to see stars as he felt the coil of arousal tighten in his groin with every thrust. With their hands still intertwined, their marks flared to life. Scott's mark sent a sensation of utter pleasure down his arm and straight down into his cock.

Looking up at Ross, Scott could tell that his mark must be doing the same thing. Looking at each other in wonder, both marks flared brightly, and they both cried out as they watched each other go over the edge, their bodies seizing simultaneously. Scott could feel every pulse of Ross' cock inside of him, as he was filled up for the first time with his soulmate's seed. His own orgasm felt like it lasted forever, even as Ross collapsed on top of him. Through the blinding pleasure, Scott could feel their bond snap into place, almost like a physical thing.

Awash with raw emotion over the experience, Scott found he was sobbing, even as Ross clung to him and was equally overcome. Slowly they came down from their orgasmic high, and Ross moved to curl up next to Scott.

Scott looked over at Ross in awe. "Wow ... that was. Wow."

"That was amazing, sweetheart. Can you feel it? The bond...?"

"Yeah, it's like something snapped into place. A piece I've been missing inside myself. I think I finally understand what the big deal is. I had no idea it could feel like this."

"Neither did I," Ross said, hugging Scott to him tightly. "I've never felt this close to anyone before. I think I'll have to keep you."

Laughing, Scott held up his left hand next to Ross' and saw that their soulmarks had completely manifested now, the pattern fully visible against their pale skin. "I think you're stuck with me, regardless."

Seeing both of their marks side-by-side, made his heart flutter, and he turned and gave Ross a slow, sweet kiss. Ross cupped his cheek and smiled. "Are you ready to face the world tomorrow, sweetheart?"

"No, but with you by my side, I'm sure I'll manage."

REGISTRATION

Ross yawned and cracked open his eyes, only to find Scott watching him. "Hey, g'morning. Been awake long?"

"As soon as the sun streamed in through those giant windows over there," Scott grumbled with a scowl which quickly turned into a smirk. "The view is even more amazing in daylight."

"Yeah, it is. That's why I love staying here sometimes," Ross said as he reached up and pulled Scott down with a yelp and kissed him fiercely. "Can you feel how much I want you again?"

Scott nodded as he felt Ross' arousal slide along his hip. Ross slid his hand down and stroked over Scott's erection. "Oh, are you hard for me, too? We don't have a lot of time, but I need you."

Scott smiled up at him while arching into Ross' hand that was slowly stroking his cock. "How about you take me in the shower?"

Ross smiled at that and kissed Scott again. "I love how you think, sweetheart."

Leading Scott to the bathroom, he kept stopping and kissing him, until Scott pushed back. "We're never going to get out of here if you keep doing that."

"Yeah, you're right. I can't help it, I'm so happy right now. I'm fully bonded with my soulmate, my soulmark is fully formed, and I had the best sex of my life last night," Ross confessed. "I didn't think you'd be so eager to get out of here?"

"I'm not. I guess I just want to get that press conference over with, like ripping off a Band-Aid," Scott explained. "Now move. You can kiss me more in the shower."

Laughing Ross conceded. "Good point."

As soon as they were in the shower, Ross pushed Scott against the wall and kissed him deeply. Scott wrapped his arms around him and pulled him close enough, so their erections slid against each other.

Breaking off the kiss with a groan, Ross reached for the bottle of lube he kept in the shower. "Turn around sweetheart. I need to be inside you."

Scott turned and bent over enough to present his ass. "Your ass is so beautiful, and it's still pink from your spanking. Fuck that's hot. I'll have to remember to use that hairbrush more often."

Scott moaned at the suggestion.

Lubing his fingers, he spread it over Scott's offered hole and then slicked up his own cock. "I'm going to open you up with only my cock. You should still be nice and loose from last night."

The needy whine that Scott made was all Ross needed to hear before he lined himself up and slid slowly back into Scott's tight heat. Ross fucked himself into Scott's hole slowly, making room for his cock along the way, until he was completely seated.

"You feel so good, sweetheart. Does it feel good when I fill you up?"

"Fuck, yes ... don't know why I avoided this for so long ... you make me feel so full ... so ... complete."

His heart fluttered to hear Scott admit that. "You complete me too, Scott. In more ways than I can say," Ross said as he slid his hands up to grip Scott's shoulders. "Go ahead and touch yourself ... I wish I could make love to you all day long, but we don't have enough time today. Do you think you can take a good hard pounding?"

Already stroking himself Scott groaned. "Yeah, please move. Fuck me! *Please?*"

"Alright, hold on," Ross warned as he gripped Scott's shoulders tight before beginning to thrust, setting a fast and brutal pace. They both moaned in pleasure, Scott practically screaming as Ross continued to pound him hard and fast.

Shouting his release, Scott tensed around him and Ross chased his own pleasure. "Fuck, sweetheart. I'm close ... I'm gonna come. Gonna fill you up so good ... fuck ... fuck ... *fuck!*"

Ross pulled Scott's hips tight against his own when his cock began to pulse, filling Scott with his seed as deep as he could get. When he was finished coming, he leaned forward over Scott's back and caught his breath.

"I could get used to this," Ross purred as he trailed kisses along Scott's neck. "You're so perfect for me."

After he'd slipped out, Scott turned in his arms and pulled him in for a lingering kiss. "I'm glad you saved my idiotic ass."

"Now that's the right attitude to have! I'll happily save you again, as many times as necessary to get the point across that you belong with me."

Scott looked down at his left hand. "Well, I think this should help remind me," he said before pulling Ross into another kiss.

Reluctantly, Ross broke the kiss sooner than he would have wanted. "We better finish getting ready. We have a registration to file before that press conference I scheduled."

"I know it can't be avoided, but I wish we could run away together and hide from the world."

"I know. Don't worry, the media attention will die down eventually, and I've got a pretty good security team in place to help avoid the worst of it."

"That's a relief," Scott said as he began to wash himself in earnest. "I'm glad you'll be with me through all of it."

"You can count on that, sweetheart."

* * *

Two hours later and Ross was leaving the Bonding Registration office with Scott. Back in the limo, they made their way to his company's headquarters, where the press conference was to be held.

"Are you ready?" Ross asked as the limo pulled to a stop.

"Not really, but I'm as ready as I'll ever be."

Taking Scott's hand, he led him inside and to the room set aside for the press conference. They made their way toward the podium and immediately cameras began flashing and snapping photos.

"Ladies and gentlemen of the press, I am here to announce that after many years of searching for my soulmate, I have found him. We finalized our bonding last night, and we came here straight from the Bonding Registration office. I am pleased to introduce my soulmate, Scott Hansen."

After relating their story of how they met, they allowed for a few more moments of photos. Then the floor was opened for questions. Ross and Scott did their best to answer them, based on the revised timeline that they had agreed on.

"Why did it take you so long to finalize your bond?"

"As you can imagine, finding out that your soulmate is of the same-sex and is someone with as much wealth and notoriety as I have, can be pretty intimidating. So, after the initial bond was formed, we agreed to take some time to get to know each other first," Ross replied.

Taking Scott's hand, he tried to encourage him to respond as well. Clearing his throat, he stepped up to the mic. "Um, yeah. Meeting Ross was overwhelming at first, but he's been patient with me. I'm so happy he's my soulmate."

They took questions for another half-hour before Ross dismissed the media. "I think that's enough questions for now. Scott and I will be doing a press tour across the country, so you can tune in to hear more."

Once the room was clear, Scott breathed a sigh of relief. "Hey, can we stop by my place, so I can grab some more of my stuff?"

"Don't worry Scott, I've already taken care of it," Ross explained. "You would be expected to move in with me immediately after the bonding registration, so I took the liberty of having some of my people clear out your apartment and cancel your lease."

"You did what!? Without even asking me?"

Turning to face Scott, Ross took a breath and gave him a stern look. "Scott, we're now bonded soulmates ... and I have told you that I am very dominant in my relationships. We discussed that it would be expected that we start living together, and I wasn't about to move into your apartment. With everything that's going on, it was more efficient for my people to pack everything up and bring it to the estate."

"I thought you said we didn't have to be *tied at the hip?* That you would let me have my own space, in case I ever needed some privacy?" Scott reminded him.

Oh shit, I did say that, didn't I? "You're right I did promise you that. I'm sorry, it slipped my mind, and I just wanted to get everything finalized before we left on our press tour," Ross apologized.

"You should have at least asked me first. I don't like strangers going through my belongings."

"I assure you, everything that they packed and moved to the estate was done with the utmost discretion and professionalism. I had everything moved into a spare suite at the estate. From there, you can take your time going through everything and deciding what to keep or what to get rid of. In fact, if you want, you could use that as your own personal suite."

Scott stared at him for a long moment. "Well, okay. I would like to have a space of my own, so thank you. But please talk to me before doing things like that first, okay?"

"I'll try. I'm not used to considering others when I make decisions."

Letting out a resigned sigh before chuckling. "I can tell. So, now what?"

"I need to run up to my office for a bit, since I've been gone so long. Then we can go back home. My staff will be back, and they'll have dinner waiting for us when we arrive. We have a couple of days to plan before we leave on the press tour."

"Alright. So, show me the office of the famous CEO of Milgrave United."

"Right this way, sweetheart."

They rode the elevator to the top floor and Ross led Scott around, introducing him to his staff on the way to his office. Once inside he watched as Scott took in the view. "The view is no surprise, but wow this is some office."

"Thanks. I spend a lot of time here, so I designed it to be comfortable," Ross said. "I might be awhile. Should I have them bring us some lunch? There's also a TV if you'd like to entertain yourself for a bit."

"If I had known, I'd have brought my laptop. I could have gotten back into my writing."

"Can you access your work from online?"

Scott shrugged. "Yeah, I guess. Everything I save gets backed up to the cloud."

Ross went over to a large built-in cabinet and opened the bottom drawer, pulling out a brand-new laptop that was still in its original packaging and handed it to Scott. "Here. Consider this a bonding gift."

Letting out a whistle as he read the specs on the side of the box, Scott looked impressed. "Wow, this is really high-end. Thanks Ross. You're starting to spoil me rotten." Scott thanked him with a kiss.

"Every chance I get," Ross teased.

Once Scott was settled in with the new laptop and he had ordered lunch, Ross powered up his own computer. There would be a backlog of emails and other things that he should catch up on while he was here. There wouldn't be much time while they were on the press tour, and he'd already spent more time away from the office than he'd originally planned.

Scanning through his email, he addressed a few of them and flagged most for later. The incessant blinking of the red light on his office phone also drew his attention, so he checked his voicemail next.

Most of the calls were check-ins from contractors working on various projects. He took notes for follow-ups where necessary and then deleted each one. The final one had been recorded a few moments after their press briefing downstairs had ended.

Clicking through to listen to the final voicemail, Ross stiffened as soon as he recognized the voice.

"Ross, old pal! It's been awhile, hasn't it? Hey, remember that prime piece of real estate you stole from me a few years ago? Well, I think I finally have an opportunity to get it back from you. Let's just say ... I know the truth behind you and this new soulmate of yours. If you don't want it made public, then you'll sign that property over to me. You have twenty-four hours."

"Shit!!"

PANIC

Scott startled when he heard Ross swear and slam the phone receiver down. He was bent over his desk, both palms supporting his weight and his face was—*shit something was wrong.*

"What happened?" Scott asked.

"Someone knows the truth about us ... about your running away from me at the party. A very dangerous someone."

"Who? How?"

"I have no idea how, but it shouldn't surprise me. As for who, he's my business rival, Stuart Grant."

"Stuart Grant? That asshole knows about us? Is he going to expose us?"

"He's threatening to, if I don't hand over some prime real estate that I managed to snag out from under him several years ago. I haven't developed it yet, but I have some big plans to redevelop the area. I could potentially lose billions if I hand that land back over to him, not to mention damaging my reputation. This could ruin me."

Fuck. It's all my fault. I did this. An overwhelming sense of panic overcame him. Without thinking, Scott ran blindly out of Ross' office. He didn't know where he was running to—or from. All he knew was that he had to get out of there. He ran past the elevators and into the stairwell, running down flight after flight. In the distance he heard Ross shouting down at him to stop but he couldn't. He had to keep running.

When he burst through the first-floor door, he ran right into Ross' arms. It hadn't occurred to him that the elevator could bring Ross down faster. "Please, let me go! It's my fault—"

"Hey, you listen to me. It's not your fault, okay? I'll figure out a way to fix this. Please, calm down."

Scott's legs gave out, and he sagged in Ross' arms. The next thing he knew he was being lifted and carried. Ross took him out to a waiting limousine. Once they were both settled inside, Ross instructed the driver. "Take us home."

Scott curled into himself and sobbed.

"Scott, take a deep breath and then I want you to come here and kneel for me."

It took a moment for Scott's mind to understand the command, before he complied. Once he was kneeling on the floor of the limo, between Ross' legs, he looked up and cringed at the stern look Ross was giving him.

"Do you remember when I asked you to tell me if you were feeling panicked, instead of running?"

"Yeah," Scott replied.

"Is that how you should address me?"

Oh ... Ross was being a Dom again. Right, the kneeling.

"No, Sir. Sorry, Sir."

"That's better."

"I will no longer tolerate such behavior, now that we're fully bonded. I'm going to give you a hand spanking now, and proper punishment when we get home."

"Yes, Sir," Scott agreed.

"Color?"

"Green, Sir."

"Good. Pull down your pants and underwear and bend over my lap."

His fingers were shaking as he complied, feeling humiliated at being bent over Ross' lap in the back of the limo where the driver could hear everything.

"Just to be clear, if you become aroused, you are not allowed to orgasm from this. If you do, I will add to your punishment later. Is that understood?"

"Yes, Sir."

This spanking was different from the one last night. The spanks were delivered with a punishing force that must have stung Ross' hand as much as it did his own ass. Nor did Ross relent until the limo drove through the security gates of the estate.

Scott's ass felt like it was on fire and he cried out at every smack. When the spanking stopped, he needed several moments to catch his breath. After the limo pulled up to the house, Ross opened the door, not waiting for the driver. "Pull your pants up and follow me."

Scott slid off Ross' lap and wiped his face on his sleeve. He winced as he pulled his pants over his abused ass. Maybe he should have said the safeword, but he lay there and took his punishment, letting the pain wash away the panic and terror that had overcome him.

Ross led them directly to the playroom. "Strip and kneel in the center of the room."

Once in place, Scott wondered what the punishment was going to be. It surprised him when Ross grabbed the spanking chair and placed it in front of him and sat down.

"Okay, before I punish you, we need to talk. Was the panic brought on by Stuart's threat?"

Scott nodded. "Yes, Sir."

"Are you worried that I'm angry with you and that I blame you for Stuart blackmailing me?"

"Yes, Sir."

"Would you believe me if I told you that I'm not angry and I don't blame you?"

Scott's breathing increased, and he lowered his eyes and shook his head. "No, Sir."

"So, you still don't trust me?"

"What? No! I didn't mean *that*. I do trust you, Ross!"

Ross' eyebrows rose as he looked skeptically at Scott. "I think I need to set some ground rules. You need more stability, and I think I need to be more consistent with how I treat you. Going between a Dom/sub dynamic and back to a more vanilla relationship is keeping you off-center. It's not helping your mental state. Would you agree?"

Thinking about it, Scott realized it did throw him every time they switched the dynamic between them from equals to ... *this*. "Yeah ... um, yes, Sir."

"Okay. We can have a longer discussion about this later, but for right now let's establish a few rules. These are temporary until we can discuss everything in more detail. First, I make all major decisions for both of us. I will talk to you first, and I will give you a voice, but once I've made the final decision, that's it. No arguments or berating me. Second, since I am making the decisions, you will not be blamed if things go wrong. Things that you have done in the past and been punished for are to be forgotten. There is no reason to panic over something you can no longer change. If you make a mistake and do something you shouldn't—like running instead of talking to me in a moment of panic—then you will be punished and forgiven."

Ross stopped speaking and Scott tried to process that for a moment. *I have to give up all control to Ross? Am I ready to commit to that?* Letting someone else make all the decisions felt freeing, but he still wrestled with the idea.

"Do you agree to those rules? Will you let me take care of you?"

"This is only temporary, right?"

"Scott, you do know that our bond will last for life? I was going to introduce you into this lifestyle a little more slowly, but it's clear to me that you need a firm hand. However, you can negotiate the rules if they aren't serving their intended purpose. We will need to discuss a more detailed protocol anyway, but I need to draw one up that's customized to our specific needs and that works for our dynamic together."

"Okay. Then I agree to those rules for now, Sir," Scott said.

Ross stood and ruffled his hair affectionately. "Good boy. Now, stand up and crawl onto the spanking bench, please. I know I warmed your ass on the ride home, but you still need a proper punishment. You'll take ten from a belt for running from me again."

Scott made his way over to the bench and crawled onto it, his hands and knees supporting him on padded ledges, while his torso lay on the center padded surface. This forced his legs apart, making him feel exposed and vulnerable. Ross then strapped him down with leather cuffs and fetched the instrument of his punishment.

"What's your color?"

Taking a cleansing breath through his nose, Scott thought about it for a moment. He already felt more at peace than he had earlier, and the thought of taking the belt didn't alarm him. "Green, Sir."

"I'd like you to count these and apologize."

The first strike from the belt hit with a flare of pain, causing Scott to cry out. After that lengthy hand spanking, he'd gotten on the ride home, his ass was already tender.

"Scott?"

"Sorry. One, Sir. I'm sorry for running again."

"Better."

Each new strike seared into his skin like a branding iron. By the time they reached the final lashes, Scott was struggling to enunciate the count through his sobs.

"Ni ... nine, S ... Sir. I'm so s ... s ... sorry."

Crack.

"Ahh! T ... Ten. Sir. Sorry ... sorry ... so sorry."

Scott's body was wracked with sobs when Ross unshackled him and pulled him into his arms. "Shh, sweetheart. It's over. You're forgiven now. You took your punishment well. I'm proud of you."

He clung to Ross as he tried to calm himself. Ross tilted his face and wiped away the tears, before giving him a brief, tender kiss.

"Come, let me take care of those welts," Ross said as he picked Scott up and cradled him in his arms. He carried him into the master bedroom and gently lay him on the bed. Scott still winced as his ass contacted the mattress, and he immediately flipped over onto his stomach.

"Don't move, I'll be right back."

Moving wasn't part of his plan right now, but Scott did grab a pillow and curl himself into a ball. He was trying to let go of the guilt, but he kept replaying that night at the party in his head over and over. If he had only reached out and took Ross' hand. If he hadn't been a coward like his dad. *If ... if ... if...*

"Hey, get out of your head or I'm putting you back over that bench," Ross teased as he came back carrying a tray. "Straighten out, please. I have some ointment for those welts."

Scott straightened out his legs, hugged the pillow, and hid his face.

"Yeah, these will bruise nicely. You'll be feeling this for a few days," Ross was saying as he gently spread the ointment on his ass. The initial touch made him hiss, but Ross' gentleness as the ointment was worked into his skin felt soothing. "Hopefully, you'll think twice before bolting like that again. Where were you running to?"

"I have no idea. I wasn't thinking. I reacted with no thought of the consequences."

Ross crawled onto the bed, still in his slacks and shirt. "Come here," he said as he opened his arms. Scott crawled up and snuggled into his soulmate's embrace. Ross held him close and kissed the top of his head.

"Scott, I know we haven't even known each other that long, but I already care about you so deeply..."

Scott's breath hitched, and he looked up at Ross. "You do?"

"Sweetheart, of course I do. We're soulmates. I know you've been struggling with it, but I do hope you'll come to care for me someday. Hopefully, you'll even learn to love me."

Scott studied Ross' face and saw the sincere emotion reflected in his beautiful eyes. Heat flooded his cheeks when he realized how much that affected him. His heart thudded loudly in his ears as he ducked his head shyly and admitted. "I ... I haven't been willing to say it out loud, but ... I do care about you."

Ross reached out and gently lifted Scott's face, caressing it. "You do? Hearing those words makes my heart soar. Are you sure you're not just saying that to appease me?"

Shaking his head, he looked into Ross' eyes, so full of hope. "No, Sir. I mean it. I have come to care for you. A spark began even before we were fully bonded, but now I'm even more certain of it."

Ross pulled Scott closer and kissed him gently. "I'm so glad to hear that. Now, let me ask, do you like calling me Sir?"

Scott nodded. "I don't know why. I had no idea I'd ever be into ... this sort of thing, but yeah, I like it."

"Can you tell me why you like it?"

Shrugging Scott shook his head. "Not really. I mean, submitting to you seems to help calm my anxiety and quiets my mind a little. Somehow, it also makes me feel closer to you."

"That's good. Would you like to keep calling me *Sir* all the time, or only when we're in the playroom?"

"Wouldn't it be weird for your soulmate to call you *Sir*?"

"No, not if that's how our dynamic works together. Those rules I was mentioning earlier, they are part of what's known as a domestic discipline partnership," Ross clarified.

Looking at Ross, everything they'd been discussing finally made sense. "Oh, that's what all this is? I'd heard of those kinds of arrangements before, but I never understood what they entailed."

"They are not uncommon between bonded soulmates, but they occur rarely with unbonded couples. I never engaged in such an arrangement with any of my past partners. I think it works best when a couple has a soulmate bond as a foundation," Ross explained. "We still need to flesh out all the details, but those are some of the basic rules in such a relationship. It goes a little beyond kinky spankings as your ass can currently attest."

"Heh, yeah. I guess I need to stop running every time I panic, because I don't think my ass can take much more, Sir."

"There are other forms of punishment, if I think your ass is at its limit. Those are the details we'll need to discuss. Knowing your soft and hard limits from that list will help. Now sit up a little. I need you to drink some juice and eat a small snack. After an intense scene like that, this will help keep you from crashing again."

"Crashing?" Scott asked as Ross stood and went over to a small mini fridge that was in one corner of the large bedroom.

"It's commonly known as *sub drop*," Ross explained when he handed Scott the bottle of juice and a small package with cheese and crackers. "It's an imbalance that can lead to a depressive state, if I don't provide aftercare when we've finished a scene. It's my job, as your Sir, to take care of you properly, so that doesn't happen. It's what you experienced after that first punishment I gave you several days ago. I shouldn't have left you alone so soon after that scene. I won't make that mistake twice."

"You don't need to be sorry, Sir. I was just overwhelmed because of everything that I'd remembered," Scott said.

"That's exactly why you shouldn't have been left alone," Ross said. "I am sorry, and it won't happen again."

"Oh, okay." Scott silently enjoyed his snack while Ross held him. "This feels nice, Sir."

"I'm glad, and I want to thank you. Focusing on you has helped me clear my own head. I think I know how to deal with Stuart now."

"Are you going to spank him too, Sir?" Scott joked.

"Metaphorically speaking ... yes I am."

DIAGNOSIS

Ross enjoyed holding Scott in his arms. Taking the time to focus on Scott's latest panic attack had helped distract him from doing a knee-jerk reaction to Stuart's threat. Now, lying here together had given him the time to think of the best way to deal with the situation.

The property that Stuart wanted him to hand over held a special significance to Ross. The land he owned included the Johnstown neighborhood where he grew up. That is why he'd bought the land when it went up for sale. He'd been taking his time to redevelop the area, because he wanted to do right by the people living there.

There was no way he could, in good conscience, hand the land back to Stuart, knowing the man was infamous for razing neighborhoods to the ground and displacing the residents. It would leave thousands of people without a home and shut down many of the small, local businesses. Giving the land to Stuart, knowing full-well what would happen, could ruin his reputation as an ethical real estate developer.

The financial consequences of that aside, it would also affect the employment of many people at his company. Personally, he could take the financial hit, but he couldn't let his employees down like that.

Ross was well known for touting the importance of large corporations working with small businesses, instead of competing against them. He also worked with local residents wherever his company developed a new project. Instead of driving people out of their homes and out of business, his goal was to help revitalize the local economy. To him, it was good business. If the local economy thrived, then so would his own business. It was unorthodox, but it had made him one of the most successful real estate developers in the country.

Stuart had given him a day, and that gave him time to plan. He had to find a way to neutralize the threat Stuart made without giving in to his demands. The good news was that nothing that he or Scott had said at their press conference was a lie. They only omitted the more damning parts of their story. What Ross had to do now was find a way to make people feel sympathetic toward their situation.

A few ideas came to mind, but Ross had to figure out the best way to spin this. That meant bringing someone else into his confidence to help pull this off. The head of his company's PR department would be a good start.

When Ross heard Scott begin softly snoring next to him, he leaned down and kissed the back of his head before extricating himself and heading to his study. He had some research to do and phone calls to make.

* * *

Several hours later, a mostly naked Scott came wandering into the study. "Hey, what are you still doing up?"

Glancing at the time, Ross rubbed his eyes. "Sorry, I didn't realize how late it was. I've been working on a plan to neutralize Stuart's threat. However, I could use your opinion since it will affect you."

"Yeah, okay," Scott agreed sitting down with a wince that made Ross smirk.

"We need to come forward with the truth, before Stuart can make it public. If it comes from us, it undermines his entire plan. The trick is that we need to spin it so people will feel sympathetic toward us, and toward you especially. I've been brainstorming ideas with the head of my PR department."

"This late? I hope you pay them overtime! Have you come up with anything?"

"Well, there's the whole angle about your dad, which I think gives you good cause to have freaked out when you met me. I also plan to bring in a professional psychiatrist to evaluate you first thing in the morning. You seem to have signs of something like PTSD because of what your dad did, and how it affected your mom and your entire childhood. If that's true, I think that would give you a huge pass on why you reacted the way you did."

Curling in on himself, Scott shook his head. "Do I have to? I can barely talk to you about it, without you spanking it out of me."

"If you need me to, I can make it an order."

"Yes, Sir. Please."

"Okay, so be it. You *will* speak with the psychiatrist that is arriving tomorrow morning. I will be with you the whole time, and I will punish you if you refuse. Right in front of the psychiatrist, if necessary."

Scott's eyes went wide, but when he noticed the stern look on Ross' face, he gave in. "Okay, fine. I'll do it, Sir."

"Lose the attitude or you'll find out how sore that ass can really get. Go back to bed and get more rest. You'll need it."

"Yes, Sir. How about you?"

"I'm too worked up right now, I don't think I could sleep if I wanted to. I may join you later after I try to wind down."

"Okay. Goodnight, Sir."

"Goodnight, sweetheart."

* * *

The next morning came far too early, but Ross managed to get a couple of hours sleep before they had to get up. He dragged Scott into the shower and they had barely finished dressing when the psychiatrist arrived. Ross was grateful his staff was back. They let the guest in and made sure they all had a cup of coffee in hand before they started.

"Thank you for making a house call on such short notice, Dr. Landry," Ross said. "I'd like to see if there is any sympathetic angle we can take, to explain why Scott fled from me when we met."

"I'm happy to help. I don't agree with the societal shaming of soulmate pairs that begin their relationship with some reluctance. I've always felt the process is very overwhelming and that not all of us are equipped to handle it. Scott, why don't you start by telling me everything you've told Ross, and we can take it from there."

Scott recounted everything, from what had happened with his parents, to his thoughts and actions after meeting Ross.

"Yesterday it happened again. Ross was so upset over being blackmailed; something that wouldn't have happened if I hadn't run from him in the first place. I panicked and fled again. Thankfully, Ross caught up with me and helped me put my head back on straight."

"How is Ross helping you?"

Ross watched as Scott's face turned several shades of red. "Well, um, you see…"

"Let me explain," Ross interjected. "Dr. Landry, for full disclosure, I practice BDSM and have been a Dom for many years. I was pleased to find that Scott has a very natural tendency toward submission. While introducing him to the lifestyle, I have also been using some techniques to help clear his head and find absolution when I notice him punishing himself."

"I see. Have you had much success?" Dr. Landry asked.

"I think we have made some progress, yes. It was my idea to use impact play—specifically a spanking—to help Scott achieve the emotional release he needed to admit to himself why he ran."

"Techniques like that can be effective, when consensual. Did you agree to this Scott?"

Scott reached over and took Ross' hand. "Yes, I did. I was skeptical that it would work, but I was willing to try. I think Ross is right about my being a natural submissive. From what we've done so far, everything feels right. I always feel so relaxed afterward, as if a burden had been lifted from me."

"Scott, would you be willing to speak with me privately? No offense to you Mr. Milgrave, but I need Scott to be able to speak with me openly, without fear of reprisal from you."

"May I share what we discuss afterward?" Scott asked.

"If you wish to discuss it with your soulmate, absolutely. That is your choice to make," Dr. Landry replied.

"Okay. I think I'm okay talking to Dr. Landry alone, Sir."

Ross squeezed his hand and stood. "Good boy. Please bring Dr. Landry to my study when you're finished."

* * *

An hour later, Scott and Dr. Landry came to find him. "Scott, please go have some breakfast. I'd like to speak with Dr. Landry alone. We can discuss everything together later."

"Yes, Sir."

"Please, sit," Ross invited. "Can I offer you anything else to drink?"

"No, I'm fine. You were right to suspect an issue. Scott is suffering from a panic disorder, which may be genetic given that his father could have also been exhibiting symptoms. I would need to run more tests to be absolutely certain of the genetic component, but you have a good case here that could garner public sympathy."

"That's a relief. Would you be willing to go on public record with that diagnosis?"

"Absolutely. Neither of you deserves to be ostracized for a condition that Scott didn't know he had until he was confronted with the one thing that could trigger it; meeting his soulmate."

"Am I doing more harm than good by trying to settle him into a domestic discipline dynamic?"

"No. What he needs right now is stability and structure, and that's exactly what domestic discipline strives to achieve."

"Yes, that's exactly the idea. Okay. I need to get out in front of this threat first, then I can focus on setting up the house rules and structure Scott will need. Can you meet me at my office building at 1 p.m.? That's when I plan to hold the next press conference."

"I'll be there, Mr. Milgrave. You can count on it."

"Thanks."

* * *

They arrived for the press conference a few minutes early. "Scott, unless they ask you a direct question, you do not need to speak. If they do ask you, be as forthright with the reporters as you were with me and Dr. Landry, okay?"

"Yes, Sir. I can do that."

Ross had also alerted his security team regarding Scott's tendency to flee. In case he panicked and ran again, they would be prepared to detain him.

As soon as Dr. Landry arrived, Ross took Scott's hand and led him before the throngs of reporters. "Welcome back. Yesterday I announced having found and bonded with my soulmate, Scott Hansen. We told you our story of how we met, but we were not entirely honest with our recounting."

A murmur rose from the crowd and Ross raised his free hand to ask for silence. "You all know how soulmate rejections are viewed by our society, especially for those of us lucky enough to find a same-sex soulmate. However, I think some circumstances should be considered before judging us. We have come before you again today to give you a full, honest recounting of our meeting, and to beg for your sympathy and understanding surrounding the circumstances behind them. To that end, I brought with an esteemed psychiatrist who has taken the time to evaluate my soulmate and hopefully shed light onto the situation."

Scott's hand kept clenching in his, while he kept taking deep breaths, struggling to breathe calmly. Ross could tell he was on the verge of another panic attack. He held Scott's hand tighter in his as he recounted the actual events of their first meeting, Scott's attempt to break the initial bond, and how Ross had saved his life and brought him home.

"So, you see, most of what we told you yesterday was the absolute truth. We left out a few details. Upon further reflection, we were afraid they may come to light in the future. We wanted to be able to tell the public the truth in our own words and have a chance to explain the circumstances."

A flurry of questions followed but Ross raised his hand again. "Before we take questions, let me first introduce Dr. Landry. He will explain to you why Scott behaved as he did. Dr. Landry?"

The doctor stepped up to the podium as Ross stepped back to make room, putting an arm around Scott's shoulders for comfort. "I met with Scott and we discussed a number of things at length. It is my professional opinion that due to a combination of genetic factors and a severe childhood trauma, that he suffers from a panic disorder. It was first triggered when he met his soulmate and he still struggles to control it. Mr. Milgrave has been doing what he can to help Scott, and I will be supervising his efforts."

Ross looked at Dr. Landry in surprise. *I didn't agree to supervision. We are going to have words about that.* They hadn't discussed this, but giving himself a moment to consider, it was probably for the best. He didn't want to risk traumatizing Scott further. Still, they were going to need to discuss the terms of whatever supervision Dr. Landry had in mind.

Dr. Landry then explained Scott's condition and why it was triggered by meeting his soulmate. Watching the reporters' reactions, he could tell that they had made the right call. The reporters' expressions had turned from mostly looks of anger and disdain, to sympathy.

There would undoubtedly still be some negative fallout, especially since they hadn't been forthright in the first place. However, Ross felt confident they wouldn't be ostracized now. Thankfully, the reporters didn't ask Scott many questions directly, especially after his first shaky response. Ross continued to hold his hand, hoping Scott wouldn't make a scene.

It wasn't until they made it back into the limousine before Ross breathed a sigh of relief. "You did well today, sweetheart. I'm proud of you. I could tell you wanted to, but thank you for not pulling away from me and running."

"Thanks for not letting go of my hand, Sir. It helped ground me."

Next, Scott did something surprising. He slid out of his seat and crawled until he was kneeling by Ross' feet. He laid his head on Ross' lap and only then did the tension he had been carrying seem to melt away.

Running his fingers through Scott's hair, Ross smiled. "Do you like kneeling for me, sweetheart?"

"Yes, Sir. Ever since that first night we tried this. I had never felt so calm before."

"Then I'll add this to our domestic discipline plan. You'll ride in the limo with me like this unless otherwise instructed. We can also sit like this together in the study on occasion, and if you need it, you can always request it from me."

"Thank you, Sir."

PLAYTIME

Scott settled into life at the estate. Now that all his belongings had been relocated, he had a space of his own he could retreat to. Ross had decided to postpone their press tour, in order to draw up the domestic discipline contract. He wanted to get Scott used to the dynamic before they headed out.

So, while Ross was busy working on the contract, Scott decided to investigate what domestic discipline entailed. It was somewhat common among bonded soulmates, but Scott had never paid much attention to how others lived their lives.

After his mom had passed, Scott buried himself in his work, only going out to soulmate parties at the behest of his publisher. It hurt his sales when people found out that he had been rarely attending them, so reluctantly he agreed to go more regularly. Even then, he didn't spend much time making more than small talk with the ladies he met. Instead, he preferred to bring them home, where they didn't do much talking at all.

From the sources he found, there was a common approach. After a soulmate couple completed their bonding and registered, they would take about a month to determine their dynamic. If it was clear that one partner was more dominant than the other, they would draw up a plan together and agree to it. There had to be a mutual agreement for it to be legally binding. The final agreement had to be reviewed by a magistrate and both parties interviewed separately before the contract could be signed.

Not all agreements included BDSM components, and commonly punishments were often loss of privileges in the home. Because of their dynamic, Scott had no doubt that Ross would include BDSM aspects into the contract. It still surprised him, but Scott was open to the idea. Everything he and Ross had done together so far had helped with his panic disorder, and he was eager to experience more of it.

The other night Ross had him try something new—*cock warming*. It wasn't something he thought he'd enjoy, but it was remarkably soothing and added a new component to an activity he already enjoyed, kneeling at Ross' feet and having his hair stroked. It meant he could give Ross something back at the same time, and he liked that.

Scott was still struggling with his newly diagnosed disorder, but Ross was being very patient with him. He was also going to continue seeing Dr. Landry in the hopes that some additional therapy may also help. As a last resort, he agreed to try medication, but Scott wanted to see if he couldn't learn to control it on his own first. Dr. Landry had prescribed some medication that he wouldn't have to take regularly but could help him in the short-term. He only had to take it if something was stressing him beyond his limit to cope, and Ross wasn't around to try other ways to calm him down. So far, he hadn't needed it.

In order to do his research undisturbed, Scott retreated to the suite that was filled with his belongings. It was almost like being back in his apartment, except for having a kitchen. Scott did insist on getting a coffeemaker for his office. He was on his second pot as he read through some of the more unusual domestic discipline arrangements. It made him wonder how far Ross would take their own contract. Scott was brought out of his reverie when a knock came to the door. When he opened it, he saw Ross standing there with a quirky grin.

"You're home early," Scott greeted, smiling back at Ross.

"We have a lot to discuss. I finished the first draft of the contract and I'd like to go over it with you. Then, if you're amenable, I want to do a trial run for a few days before we finalize it," Ross suggested.

"That sounds like a good idea. I was going to prep for my next novel, but all I've been doing is researching domestic discipline," Scott admitted with a blush. "Now is as good a time as any for me to call it quits for the day."

Shutting down his laptop and turning off the lights, Scott followed Ross to his study, where he handed him a copy of the contract. He sat down and read through it while Ross went off to make some drinks and check with the staff on dinner. Most of it read like the standard domestic discipline contracts he'd seen online, but there were a few differences. *Daily maintenance spankings? That sounds hotter than it has a right to be.*

As Ross returned with the drinks, Scott looked up from the contract. "I get the feeling you enjoy warming my ass, if this contract is any indication," Scott said with a smirk.

"I have a sadistic streak a mile wide," Ross admitted. "Is that a problem?"

"Will the daily maintenance spankings be administered as hard as the punishment ones I've received so far?"

"No. They are meant to be a reminder and help ground you, not as punishment."

Well, clearly my cock is on board with that, Scott thought as he felt his blood rushing south.

"Okay, and about the chastity and orgasm denial punishments? How do those work?"

"I was hoping you'd ask," Ross said with a sly grin. "I can't always punish you through pain. You need to heal, and I never want to break skin or cause serious injury. So, occasionally other forms of punishment will be required. I was thinking we could try that during our trial period, so you get an idea of what it's like before deciding if it's a hard limit or not. What do you think?"

"Trying it first seems like a good idea," Scott agreed. "Can we delay that until tomorrow? Since I wasn't expecting it, I'd like to have one more orgasm before that happens, please. If that's okay with you, Sir?"

"Fair enough, since it won't be done as punishment ... *this time*. How do you feel about the other rules and expectations?"

How did I get from fleeing from this man, to agreeing to let him control most aspects of my life, and why does the idea make me so hard?

"I ... I'd say they're fair," Scott replied, his voice going husky with his increasing arousal. "Especially considering my panic disorder. The stability this proposes is something I need in my life. I never even thought about it, but I guess I did keep a consistent schedule before I met you. I wasn't even aware it was something I needed."

Standing up and walking over toward him Ross knelt in front of Scott and caressed his face. "I'm pleased to hear you say that.

I hope you know I want this not only because of my personal needs, but because I care about you. I want the best for you."

Scott nodded, feeling a swell of emotion. "I know you do. I can feel it through our bond. I am falling for you more every day. A part of me is still afraid that I'll cause you more harm than good. That you're too good for me and you'd be better off without me. I guess maybe that's why my dad ran off too. My mom was an amazing woman. He probably thought he wasn't good enough for her ... for us."

"The fact you recognize that is a huge step. Thank you for sharing that. Now, shall we have dinner and then go have some fun?" Ross asked with a wink.

* * *

After dinner, they made their way upstairs. Heading into the playroom, Scott remembered the rule and immediately removed his clothes.

"Good boy. I promised you an orgasm before we try out how well you can handle being in chastity, but I want to make it interesting. Do you trust me, sweetheart?"

"Yes, Sir. I trust you."

Watching as Ross crossed the room and pressed a button in the wall he hadn't noticed before, he saw chains being lowered from the ceiling. "I'm going to cuff your hands above your head and cuff your legs to the floor. This will be a very vulnerable position for you, so if you start to panic, let me know immediately."

Picturing what Ross described made Scott shiver with excitement. There was a small frisson of fear, but no panic yet. "Yes, Sir."

"What's your color?"

"Green, Sir."

Next, the leather cuffs were put onto his wrists and ankles before Ross led him under the hanging chains. "Raise your arms for me."

With his arms raised, Ross secured each to the chains over his head. "Grab onto the chains with your hands. That will give you more stability and reduce the risk of injury to your wrists."

Taking Ross' word for it, Scott wrapped his hands around the chains. Once he had a good grip, Ross squatted before him and spread his legs apart until they could reach the large eyehooks in the floor where he clipped in the ankle restraints. Completely immobilized now, Scott's heart rate increased, and the blood seemed to rush south as he felt his cock already start to harden. *I must be a masochist. This is turning me on so much.*

"Are you already getting hard for me? Fuck, you're amazing. I'm going to make sure you come so hard tonight, sweetheart," Ross said before grabbing his face and kissing him passionately.

Stepping out of his range of vision, Ross left Scott hanging, literally. His heart hammered in his chest and his cock was already aching when Ross returned, cupping his ass and kissing his shoulder.

"This might be a little cold," was all the warning Scott got before something cold, hard, and wet was slipped between his ass cheeks. "Relax sweetheart, open up for me."

Willing himself to relax, the object was slowly inserted into his rectum until it was fully seated. "Good boy."

Coming back around to face Scott, Ross had a wicked grin as he held up a small remote, clicking one button. Scott cried out when the plug in his ass began to vibrate. "Fuck!"

"That comes later," Ross said with a wink. "First, I want to warm your beautiful skin with a flogger."

Ross showed Scott the flogger before running it over his bare skin. It made him shiver even as the vibrations continued inside of him. Ross ran the tails of the flogger gently over his chest, trailing it down over his stomach, teasing his aching cock. Then he moved behind Scott and did the same over his shoulders and down his buttocks.

"What's your color?" Ross purred into his ear.

"Very green, Sir."

When the first strike came, Scott yelped in surprise. Where the tails of the flogger hit, his skin tingled with a spreading warmth. Ross began to strike his skin again and again, over the broad expanse of his back, buttocks and thighs. Then he came around and struck Scott's chest, stomach, and the front of his thighs, while pausing to tease his cock with soft caresses of the flogger. All the while the plug kept vibrating, driving Scott crazy. He was driven to the very edge of orgasm but couldn't quite make it over the precipice.

"You already look so debauched. It's a beautiful sight. What's your color now?"

"It's still green, Sir. Please, let me come. Please, I need it."

"Oh, no, not yet. You get to come on my cock later, but I'm nowhere near done with you yet. Can you take a few strikes from a paddle on that beautiful ass of yours?"

"Yes, Sir. Please, Sir."

Ross put the flogger away and returned with a large wooden paddle. It felt cool on his heated skin as it was smoothed over his ass. "Count for me and don't come. If you come before I fuck you, I'll add an extra day to your time in chastity. Do you understand?"

"Yes, Sir. I understand. I'll try not to come."

The first strike hurt so good, Scott's cry was a mix of pain and pleasure. "One, Sir."

Ross continued to paddle his ass while Scott counted. Dozens of blows rained down as the vibrations in his ass continued. When Scott was close to coming, he cried out. "Yellow! Please, I'm too close. *Please*."

Stopping immediately, Ross also turned off the vibrator before moving behind Scott, wrapping his arms around him and leaving a trail of kisses up his neck. "You're so good for me. You're absolutely perfect. I think you deserve a reward."

"Thank you, Sir. Please, let me come."

"Soon, sweetheart. Hang on a little longer," Ross said with a chuckle.

After putting the paddle away Ross stretched and slipped a cock ring over Scott's throbbing erection.

"What? No! Sir, *please!*?" Scott whined.

"Hush. This will help make your orgasm even better. Trust me," Ross said with a light slap on his heated ass.

Taking several deep breaths, Scott nodded. "Okay. Yes, Sir."

Releasing him from his bonds, Ross helped Scott over to one of the benches in the room. He knelt over the padded surface with his ass presented at the perfect height for Ross to fuck.

"Your ass is such a beautiful shade of red," Ross praised as he ran his hands over the abused flesh. "Are you ready for my cock?"

"Yes, Sir. *Please.*"

"I can't say no when you beg me so sweetly," Ross said, pulling the plug out, leaving Scott feeling empty. He couldn't help the whine that escaped his throat. "Hush, I'll give you what you need."

Ross had remained fully clothed. Scott heard him lower his zipper and slick his cock before feeling Ross' hands on his hips. Then Ross was pushing into him in a long, slow glide, filling him up so perfectly. Ever since they bonded, he'd become addicted to having Ross fuck him. He almost felt incomplete without Ross' cock up his ass. Scott loved the frequent reminders of how perfectly they fit together.

Grasping his hips firmly, Ross began pounding into Scott. "That's it, take my cock. Fuck, you're so hot and tight for me. You may come whenever you need to sweetheart, but remember, I won't stop fucking until I come too."

He didn't care. Scott needed to come so badly his cock almost hurt with how hard he was. He ached for release. When Ross began to thrust right into his prostate, Scott rode the wave until the crescendo of pleasure washed over him. His orgasm hit him hard, coming from deep inside in a way he hadn't experienced before. He cried out as the pleasure ripped through him.

Scott was momentarily confused. His cock was still hard, and he hadn't felt it spurt like he normally did when he had an orgasm. *What the hell? Did I come?*

"That's it, Sweetheart. I love feeling you clench around me like that," Ross growled.

True to his word, Ross kept chasing his own pleasure. Scott wasn't sure how, but a mix of increased pleasure and sensitivity began to merge, making him whimper.

"I'm almost there, sweetheart. Can you come for me again? You're still hard," Ross observed as he gave him several rough strokes.

Did I come, or didn't I? What is going on … oh, fuck!

The sensitivity diminished as Ross kept stroking him, and Scott felt the pleasure coil in his groin again. As Ross' thrusts came faster and harder, another wave of pleasure crested over Scott and this time his balls drew up and his cock exploded, pumping his seed all over the bench and the floor below.

As Scott screamed his second orgasm, Ross was thrown over the edge and his hips stuttered as he rutted deep, his cock spurting inside Scott, filling him with his own release.

Several long minutes passed as Ross simply bent over and peppered kisses across Scott's back, while catching his breath. When he slid out and slipped off the cock ring from Scott he asked. "How do you feel, sweetheart? Was that worth it?"

"Yeah … um, yes, Sir. That was incredible. What happened? The first time, I came, but I didn't?"

"You had an anal orgasm. I thought we would have to work up to you being able to experience those, and here you are having one without even knowing it. You're amazing."

Scott felt so loose and relaxed after his orgasms while his skin buzzed pleasantly from all the stimulation. He heard Ross tidying up behind him, but he was too lax to care. Then Ross slid his arms around Scott and helped him up. "Come on, let's go take a bath."

Scott hissed as his abused skin first submerged in the hot, soapy water. It took a few moments for the sting of it to fade as he leaned back onto Ross who sat behind him. Ross wrapped his arms around Scott and held him, kissing his neck, suckling marks that would certainly bruise.

Laughing, he remembered his first hickey he got back in high school. "What's so funny, sweetheart?"

"Oh, I remembered when this girl and I were making out years ago. I must have been ... fourteen, maybe fifteen? She started sucking on my neck and when it left a bright red mark, she was terrified. She thought she was going to get in trouble for doing that to me."

"That's cute. I want the world to see you wear my marks and know that you belong only to me now."

Turning in Ross' arms, Scott looked to see the depth of affection in his eyes. "I know it doesn't always seem like it, but I am very glad to be yours. It already feels like I've known you all my life. I guess what they say is true. Soulmates will always know each other, no matter how old they are when they finally meet."

Ross slid a hand over his cheek, stroking his thumb before pulling Scott in for a soft, tender kiss. "You know how deeply I care about you, Scott. I've felt a connection to you from the moment I laid eyes on you."

Emotion coiled in Scott's chest and he blinked back the burn from freshly formed tears. "I know I'm falling for you, Sir. I ... I'm not ready to let myself fall all the way yet. I do care about you—"

"It's enough, for now."

CAGED

Ross was elated how close he and Scott had become. Scott may not be ready to declare his love yet, but it thrilled Ross to know that he was starting to fall for him. It meant their soulmate bond was strong, and they were truly compatible. His domination over Scott helped balance them both, and it served to strengthen their bond even further.

Today he'd made plans to begin the trial run of their domestic discipline contract. They needed to finalize the details before the planned press tour that had already been delayed longer than was probably wise, but necessary under the circumstances.

Once they were done with their morning shower, Ross led Scott back to the bedroom. "I'm going to put you into chastity now, so please lay down on the bed, on your back."

"Yes, Sir."

Going into his closet, Ross pulled out the box that contained the custom chastity cage he had ordered for Scott. *Thank goodness for express delivery.*

"I had this custom made for you, sweetheart. It may seem a bit extreme, but I want you to get the idea of what a punishment like this entails."

Taking the cage out of its box, he showed it to Scott. It was stainless steel and shaped like a cage with rings to encase the penis. Beside it in the box was a small padlock and a long metal pin. "The largest ring will go around your scrotum to hold it in place, and this," Ross lifted the pin, "is a urethral plug."

Scott swallowed nervously. "Does that go where I think it does?"

Ross gave him a wicked grin and continued. "We're going to try this for at least twenty-four hours, although I may extend that to seventy-two," he explained as he took some lube to slick the plug. "I know we haven't talked about this part, but this punishment doesn't only control your erections and orgasms. It also controls when you get to urinate. While wearing this, you will need to ask my permission any time you need to use the bathroom."

Scott's eyes shot wide at that and he looked like he was about to protest. "Let me explain. As the name implies, this plug goes into your urethra. It attaches to the cage and is screwed closed at the tip. It's hollow, and when the cap is removed, you will be able to pee through it. This will not need to be removed and re-inserted every time, okay?"

Scott nodded, although doubt still clouded his face.

"I'm going to slide it in now and then check on you before putting on the cage. If it's too much, we can try it again another time."

"Okay, Sir," Scott agreed cautiously.

"Good boy," Ross praised. "Try not to get hard."

"I'll try, Sir."

Ross took Scott's flaccid penis in one hand and the lubed plug in the other. Slowly he fed it into the tip of Scott's cock. When Scott made an uncomfortable hiss, he paused. "What's your color?"

"Green Sir. It feels ... weird."

"Okay, weird is expected. Let me know if there's any pain. I don't want to hurt you."

Scott let out a snort, muttering something under his breath.

"Did I say something funny?"

"Oh, sorry Sir. After last night ... well, my ass is still sore."

"Let me rephrase that. I don't want to injure you. I never want to do something that would cause you to bleed, or worse, need to go to a hospital. Yes, I enjoy giving you pain, but I never want to *hurt* you. Do you understand?"

The look of contrition on Scott's face was enough. "Yes, Sir. I'm sorry."

"Okay take a breath and relax for me, so I can slide the rest of this in."

Once the plug was fully seated, only the tip of it peeking out at the end of Scott's cock, Ross paused to give Scott a moment to get used to the sensation. "You took that very well. Will you be able to keep that in for a day?"

"It still feels weird, but it doesn't hurt. I think I can take it."

"Good boy. Let's get the cage on then."

Ross picked up the cage, slid it into place, pulling Scott's balls through the largest ring in the back. The rest of the cage fit over Scott's cock, with the tip of the plug peeking through the end. Then Ross screwed the cap onto the plug, effectively blocking it. The final step was locking it in place. Once locked, he removed the tiny key and put it onto the same key chain that held the key to the playroom.

"It looks good on you, sweetheart. What's your color?"

"Still green, Sir," Scott said as he moved to get up, but Ross put his hand on his chest to keep him in place. "I'd like to add one more thing, if you're up for it?"

"What is it, Sir?"

"I'd like you to wear an anal plug. It will keep you open and ready for me to take you, anytime I want. Would you try that for me?"

When he saw Scott's caged cock twitch at the idea, it made him smirk. "I'll try it, Sir."

Going back to the closet, he pulled out another box and pulled out the plug. It was also stainless steel, with an oblong loop for a base. "This one is designed specifically for long-term wear. Obviously, it would be removed whenever you need to use the bathroom, but otherwise you should be able to wear it around the clock. Raise your legs for me, let me see that pretty hole of yours."

Scott flushed red from his chest to his ears as he complied. His ass was still rosy from the previous night's activities, but his hole didn't look inflamed. Slicking up the plug, he gently pressed against Scott's anus. "Relax and let it in, sweetheart."

Once it popped in past the tight ring of muscle and settled to the base of the plug, Ross stood and helped Scott to stand, pulling him into a deep kiss. "I'm so proud of you Scott. You took all of that wonderfully. Go look at yourself in the mirror. See how good you look."

Going into the bathroom, Scott checked out the cage in the mirror. He touched it gingerly, lifting it, testing how well it was locked in place. "It does look kind of cool."

"See, I knew you'd love it. I am staying home today. Do you want to stay nude and spend time with me or do you need to get some writing done?"

"I can probably take a day off, but with the press tour coming up, I shouldn't."

"How about this? Go slip on some sweats and spend a few hours after breakfast working on your novel. Then come find me at lunchtime. We can hang out and play video games after we eat."

"That sounds like a good idea. Can I text you if I need to pee or should I come find you?"

"Well, since this isn't for an actual punishment, text me. All you'll need to do, once I give you permission, is unscrew the cap."

"If I don't text and ask you, what happens? Will you know?"

"I have sensors in every bathroom, so yes, I'll know. Then I'll have to give you a real punishment. Some lashes with a belt perhaps, or I could introduce you to the loopy johnny," Ross said with a wink and another wicked grin.

Rolling his eyes, Scott laughed. "Fine. I'll ask you when I need to pee. *Sir.*"

"That's my good boy."

*　*　*

Scott took to wearing the cage better than Ross had expected. That evening Ross led Scott to the bedroom and admired his soulmate as he undressed. The sight of the cage hanging heavy between his legs began to stir Ross' own primal urges. He walked over to Scott and wrapped his arms around him, giving him a quick kiss. "Thank you for taking the cage so well. Now you should have an idea of what a punishment like this might be like. If I were actually punishing you, you'd be trapped in that cage for a week or longer, depending on the infraction."

"Yeah, I remember, Sir. It's spelled out in explicit detail in that contract of yours."

"Are you okay with it remaining as one form of punishment?"

"Yes, Sir. I both kind of hate and love it at the same time. I keep surprising myself with how much I'm into all these kinks."

"You're my soulmate. I never had any doubt you'd be the kinky better half I'd been searching for. Now, I want you to experience the other side of this punishment … getting fucked while not being able to get hard."

"This is the orgasm denial part you mentioned, right? What if I have another one of those anal orgasms?"

"You have permission tonight, if you do. However, if you don't have an anal orgasm, then you will wait until the cage comes off. I'll make it worth your while, when the time comes."

"Okay, that sounds fair."

"Now get on the bed so I can ravish you, my love."

A look flitted over Scott's face at the new term of endearment but said nothing. He crawled onto the bed and lay down, letting Ross spread his legs. The look of Scott's caged cock was such a turn-on, Ross was hoping he'd have to punish him like this occasionally. "Fuck, this cage looks so good on you."

Leaning down, Ross kissed all around the cage before kissing and licking his balls, causing Scott to groan. With a last lick and a kiss to the cage, Ross crawled over Scott, worshipping him with his lips and tongue along the way.

Sliding his hands under Scott's arms so he could grasp his shoulders, Ross plundered his mouth while he rutted his cock in the crook of his leg.

"Do you want me, sweetheart?"

"Yes, please. I need you more than that plug."

Kissing Scott one more time, he knelt up and grabbed the lube. Sliding the plug out of Scott's ass, he slicked his cock before lining himself up and sliding in.

"Oh yes, that plug helped keep you nice and open. I'm sliding in here like I belong."

"You do belong. Right here. Fuck, you fill me up so perfectly, Sir," Scott moaned.

"That's what I like to hear. You're so hot inside. It feels so good."

Ross let himself fall forward, catching himself on his elbows before he collapsed onto Scott. He began to slide his cock in and out, taking his time, relishing the hot grip that massaged him perfectly. Scott slid his arms around his neck and pulled him down, kissing him hard, while wrapping his legs around his waist.

Changing the angle of his hips, Ross knew Scott was seeking the same release he'd had the other day. When Scott keened with pleasure, Ross knew he had gotten the angle right. That's when Ross knew to start pounding into him, hitting his prostate on every thrust.

Arching his back in ecstasy, he cried out every time Ross nailed that spot inside of him. "Can you come for me? Even with your dick locked up tight, can you come just from my cock pounding your ass?"

Snapping his hips harder, Ross knew he wasn't going to last much longer. "I'm getting close, sweetheart. I'm gonna fill you up so good."

The coiling of pleasure tightened in his gut and soon Ross was thrusting with wild abandon, chasing his own release. Scott's noises of pleasure were bordering on frustration, but Ross was nearing the point of no return. Another minute of hard, fast thrusts and Ross came. He pushed his cock until his hips were flush with Scott's and he pulsed his release deep into him, while Scott whimpered with disappointment.

Breathing hard, Ross smirked at Scott. "Don't worry, I'll make sure you have an amazing orgasm once that cage comes off."

"I know, but I really wanted to feel that anal orgasm again."

Kissing Scott tenderly, Ross winked at him. "*Well*, we could go for another round once I've recovered, and try again?"

Scott pulled Ross in for another kiss. Ross savored Scott's soft, plush lips on his. He relaxed into Scott's embrace and they kissed for a long while. Reaching down, he fondled the cage and Scott's balls, making him groan. The sound went straight to Ross' cock.

"Do you think you can take me again, sweetheart?"

Arching into Ross' touch Scott nodded. "Yes, please, Sir."

"Let's try it with you on your elbows and knees this time," Ross suggested, helping Scott turn around. "Put your ass up nice and high for me."

Grabbing some lube, Ross slicked himself up to full hardness before plunging back into Scott's tight heat. Since he had come once already, the same urgency he had earlier was diminished. Instead, he focused on the simmering pleasure as he slowly worked himself in and out, trying to hit Scott's prostate on every stroke.

Bending over and wrapping his arms around Scott, Ross rutted into him while his soulmate moaned in ecstasy. "That's it, sweetheart, relax and let it come. I know you're close."

Scott keened as Ross hit his prostate hard every few thrusts. "Yeah ... so close ... please ... don't stop. *Please...*"

Ross kept up the steady pace until he felt Scott clench around him, crying out as his body shuddered in ecstasy. Only then did Ross speed up his thrusts and chase his own orgasm. Scott's hole continued to clench and flutter around him, driving Ross quickly over the edge. Soon he was balls-deep, pumping another load into Scott before collapsing next to his soulmate.

Once he'd caught his breath, Ross looked over at Scott and laughed, seeing that he looked even more wrecked than he felt.

"So, was the reward worth the torment?"

"Definitely," Scott nodded with a giddy smile.

PRESS TOUR

Scott collapsed on the hotel bed as soon as they arrived. The press tour hadn't even started, and he was already exhausted.

"Don't tell me you want to get fucked again?" Ross teased as he carried in their suitcases.

"Travel wears me out," Scott complained. "I love that you have a private jet, but I've never flown on something that small before."

"Yeah, I saw you white knuckled when we took off, which is why I tried to *distract* you. One of the other perks of owning a private jet."

"Well, I'm finally a member of the mile-high club!" Scott joked with a yawn. "Now all I want to do is take a nap."

Checking his watch Ross rolled his eyes. "You can rest for an hour, but then we have to go to our first media engagement. Don't forget, afterward I have that late dinner with clients."

"Do I need to go with you for that? The hotel has room service."

"Yes, you do. After our public confession, how would it look if I arrived at a restaurant without my soulmate at my side? No one would believe how sincerely sorry you are for fleeing from me. You're going."

"Yes, Sir."

Curling onto his side, Scott closed his eyes and tried to get some rest. He couldn't fall asleep, his mind kept recounting everything that had happened in the last few days. He and Ross had finalized the details on their contract and brought it before a magistrate. It was approved and signed. Now Scott was expected to abide by the terms of that contract all the time. Ross wasn't just his soulmate, now he was officially his *Sir*. Every time he thought about that, Scott felt a mix of comfort and excitement.

Before it had been finalized, they discussed it all in detail after their trial period. Ross had been very reasonable and removed a couple of rules that Scott wasn't comfortable with. The one they argued the most about was a stipulation that Scott should ask permission every time he left the house. Ross feared Scott fleeing again and disappearing much like Scott's own father had.

As a compromise, Scott agreed to wear a GPS tracker embedded under his skin. Ross' doctor had come by before they were about to leave for the airport to embed the little device. Ross insisted it be embedded on his back where he couldn't easily reach it.

The intention of the contract was to help bring some much-needed stability to Scott's life. He knew he was calmer when his life was structured, knowing exactly what was expected of him, and understanding the consequences of his actions. They both hoped it would help him not panic as often.

What worried Scott now that the contract was in place, was that they didn't have time to ease into it at home. They had to leave almost immediately to go on this damnable press tour. Scott didn't understand what made them so special. They were two dudes who were destined to fuck and fall in love, instead of a guy and a gal. Yeah, same-sex soulmates were rare, but he never understood why they were held up on a pedestal. Traveling across the country to talk to the media and letting people gawk at them, it was like they were a couple of unicorns being put on display.

His mind drifted back to the contract. With it now in place, Ross had the right to bend him over his knee and spank him, anytime, anywhere. If he was out of line, he knew Ross wouldn't hesitate to drag him off to the nearest dark corner and warm his ass. Scott chuckled to himself when he felt his dick twitch at that thought.

Scott was trying not to be nervous about their first interview, but he couldn't help worrying about any accusatory questions they might ask him. They hadn't been ostracized and Ross managed to thwart Stuart's blackmail attempt, but there had still been some backlash. His book sales took a nosedive once people found out he was the author. The publisher also gave him a stern talking to regarding the situation.

Apparently, he'd missed a *golden opportunity* to capitalize on his rare soulmate pairing and there was a chance his career as an author was over. At least under his current name. The publisher had floated the idea of him starting over under a new pen name. He told them he'd think about it.

What felt like only a moment later, Ross shook him. "Come on, sweetheart, time to freshen up. We need to go soon."

Blinking away the grogginess as best as he could, he got up to take a quick shower. Walking out of the bathroom with just a towel around his waist, Scott looked at an expectant Ross who was seated on the edge of the bed with a hairbrush in his hand. *Oh, right. The maintenance spankings.*

"Hurry up, or we'll be late for the interview," Ross said, patting his lap. "You know this helps to ground you. If you start to panic, just focus on the soreness in your ass instead."

"Yes, Sir," Scott obeyed, dropping the towel before bending over Ross' knees.

The spanking was quick and efficient, as Ross peppered his ass with quick blows with the back of the brush. It left a lingering sting but not enough to be seriously painful like his punishments. Rubbing his ass a bit after it was over, Scott went to get dressed. Once ready, Ross led him out of the hotel and to a waiting car. "I know you're anxious. Keep holding my hand, focus on your freshly spanked ass, and let me do most of the talking. It's going to be fine."

"I'll do my best, Sir."

"I know you will. Be my good boy," Ross said as he squeezed Scott's hand.

Their first interview was a radio broadcast, so at least they wouldn't be on camera. It still made Scott nervous, but he was grateful people wouldn't be looking at his face and judging every move or facial expression.

After they arrived, they were given a brief explanation for what to expect before being led into the room where the interview would be held. They were given each a set of headphones and were sat in front of large microphones. As Scott sat, he winced slightly as he was reminded of how freshly spanked his ass was.

Their interviewer was the well-known radio talk show host, Marvin Specter. He shook both of their hands before sitting down and starting the show.

"Hello and welcome everyone to a special edition of the Marvin Spector Soulmate Hour. We have some very special guests with us today, the newly bonded same-sex soulmate couple, Ross Milgrave and Scott Hansen. Welcome, gentlemen!"

"Thank you. It's an honor to be here," Ross replied.

"Yeah, thanks," Scott chimed in, squeezing Ross' hand.

"Let's get right to the dirt so we can get it out of the way. Your second press conference blew everyone away, but what's surprising is how little backlash you two have received over your public confessions. Why do you think that is?"

"I'd like to think it's because people are feeling sympathetic to Scott's circumstances. Because of his childhood background, it wasn't easy for him to come to terms with having me as his soulmate. I'm very proud of him for working with me on his issues and getting past the worst of his anxiety."

"Scott, can you tell our viewers what's caused this panic disorder that you've been diagnosed with?"

Scott felt his heart rate pick up as he broke into a cold sweat. He knew he'd be asked to talk about this. However, being faced with it started to trigger the terror inside of him again. Ross reached out and rubbed his back, leaning over and whispered in his ear. "You can do this. Take a breath."

Nodding, Scott filled his lungs with a couple of cleansing breaths while squirming in his seat. That brought back the tender reminder of his spanking, and his nerves calmed. "Uh, yeah, okay. It's because of what happened to my parents. They were a soulmate pair and when my dad found out my mom was pregnant, for some reason ... he ran off. He left my mom to raise me alone. It broke her heart.

"She loved me the best that she could, but I always felt like a part of her blamed me for losing her soulmate. She was distant, and I remember hearing her cry herself to sleep every night. I didn't know how to fix it or how to help her. It made me afraid of finding a soulmate, especially a male one. When I met Ross, I was immediately terrified. I was afraid of what happened to my mom would happen to me, so I ran."

"You do see the irony in doing that, don't you?" Marvin asked.

Scott nodded and was prodded by Ross to speak. "Yeah ... yes, I do. After Ross pointed it out, I felt so ashamed. I'm ... I'm so sorry. Ross has been amazing, and I wish I hadn't caused so much trouble."

"Your sincere contrition seems to have melted the hearts of the people," Marvin observed before moving on to another topic. "How has your relationship been since you consummated your bond?"

"I am very happy that Scott is my soulmate. Our dynamic is everything I could have ever hoped for. In fact, before leaving for this press tour, we entered into a formalized domestic discipline contract."

"Wow," Marvin marveled. "Based on Scott's history, I bet that helps keep him in line. Does he require frequent discipline?"

Laughing Ross shook his head. "No, Scott's my good boy. I do enjoy warming his ass for other reasons, but he hasn't required punishment that often. He is very eager to please."

"How did you feel when Ross proposed such a contract to you?" Marvin asked.

"I knew they were fairly common among bonded soulmates, but I never gave them any thought before meeting Ross. I liked the concept once he explained it to me. I never realized until I met Ross how much of a natural submissive I am. Letting him make all the day-to-day decisions takes a huge weight off my shoulders and lets me focus more on my writing."

"I've heard that your novel sales have gone down since the public confession. Do you plan to continue writing?"

"I would love to, but my publisher isn't so sure anymore. Writing is my passion, so I'm not sure what else to do if I can't write anymore."

"You run a large, successful business, don't you Ross? Would Scott have a place there?" Marvin pondered.

Looking at Ross with curiosity, Scott hadn't even contemplated that possibility. "If he wanted to work at Milgrave United, I'm sure I could find him something to do, but as he said, writing is his passion. I'm hoping his readers will find it in their hearts to forgive him and buy the new novel he's been working on. I'll finance the publishing of it myself if I have to."

"Wow, really?" Scott interjected, forgetting they were speaking to an audience of millions for a moment. Ross turned to him and caressed his cheek. "Yes, sweetheart. Really."

"You are a very supportive man. I think you're putting the rest of us to shame by that admission," Marvin teased. "It's very clear how much affection you have for each other. I can see why the public has responded to you the way that they have."

They were asked several other questions before the interview was wrapped up. As they made their way back to the limo, Ross slid an arm around Scott's waist and hugged him close. "I'm proud of you. You did very well, and you only looked like you wanted to bolt once."

"It helped that Mr. Specter seemed supportive of us. I was terrified that he'd say nasty things to me, but he didn't. That helped a lot."

"Are you ready for dinner? If you make it through the next couple of hours, I promise I'll spoil you rotten when we get back to the hotel."

Scott planted a peck on Ross' cheek. "You already spoil me rotten. I'm hungry, so as long as I don't have to say much, I think I'll be fine."

They arrived at the restaurant and were led to their seats. The clients were already seated at the table. They were all older looking men, who raked their eyes up and down at Scott for a moment before looking at Ross.

"I'm sorry we're late, gentlemen. We had to complete our first interview of our press tour," Ross apologized.

"Yes, we know. We listened in while we were waiting. The host was very *tolerant* of your situation."

"He was, which I was grateful for," Ross said. "Let me introduce you to my soulmate, Scott."

Scott forced a smile as he greeted them. "Hello, nice to meet you."

The oldest of the men sitting at the table scowled at him. "I'm surprised you brought him to dinner. I figured you'd keep him chained to your bed after that stunt he pulled."

Scott felt himself tense at the hostile remark, and Ross immediately grabbed his hand.

"I do not appreciate your tone. Where I take my soulmate is none of your concern. We are fully bonded and there is no need for such vulgar suggestions."

The man snorted in derision. "If he were my soulmate, I'd be beating him to within an inch of his life every night, so he would remember his place."

"I thought we were here to discuss business, not advocate for domestic abuse, Stan?" Ross asked sternly.

"You're right, of course," Stan capitulated.

Ross took a seat while Scott stood frozen, trying to breathe as a conflict of emotions warred within him. He was trying to remain calm, but he wasn't sure he could sit idly by and let this man speak about him like that. Ross grabbed his hand again. "Sit down sweetheart, and I'll order us some drinks."

Taking a deep breath, Scott sat, trying not to glare at Stan and the other men across the table. His instinct to flee was thrumming under his skin, but he managed to keep it in check. When their drinks arrived, he gratefully took a long sip, hoping to take the edge off his nerves.

The conversation turned to the business Ross had come to discuss and Scott was thankful to be ignored. Ross ordered dinner for them both, and Scott remained silent.

The rest of the dinner went smoothly until dessert arrived. They had concluded whatever business discussions they needed to have, and Stan decided he wanted to goad Ross more regarding his soulmate.

"So, I'm curious, how much did you have to discipline him in order to get him so complacent? I'm impressed with how well you have him in-hand," Stan remarked.

Scott could see Ross bristle at the comment. "I warn you for the last time, Stan. Stay out of my personal affairs."

"If you don't wish me to discuss him, next time don't bring him along. You're lucky you've gotten him so well trained, or I might have had second thoughts about our future business dealings," Stan continued. "How you handle a problematic soulmate reflects on you in all ways, not only personal."

Anger, frustration, and so many other emotions erupted from Scott all at once. "I am not *just* some piece of furniture, you fucking, self-centered piece-of-shit! If you have a problem with me, talk to *me*!"

As soon as the words left his mouth, Scott's hands flew up to cover it. *Shit. Did he ruin Ross' business deal?* Looking at Ross he quickly apologized. "I'm sorry, Sir. I ... I don't know what came over me. Please, forgive me."

"We'll discuss it when we get home," Ross said calmly.

He didn't call me sweetheart. Oh shit. I'm in trouble. Panic rose in his throat, making it difficult to breathe. Before Ross could grab a hold of him, Scott shot up from his chair and fled the restaurant. He ran down the street, not looking where he was going. He ran until he couldn't run anymore, tears streaming down his face.

Breathing hard, he leaned against the building he'd stopped at. *Fuck, I did it again. I promised to talk to Ross before running. I'm such a failure.*

He had no idea how far he had run, or where he was. Taking out his phone he decided to call for a ride to take him back to the restaurant, ignoring Ross' calls until then. He'd rather apologize to Ross face-to-face.

When the car arrived, Scott got into the back seat and gave the driver the name of the restaurant. It wasn't until they had been driving for some time that Scott realized something was wrong. "Hey, shouldn't we be there by now? I know I couldn't have been this far away from the restaurant."

"Sit back and relax, Mr. Hansen, you'll be at your destination soon."

"Hey, wait when did I give you my name?"

That's when Scott heard the distinct click of all the car doors locking, and a partition raised between him and the driver. Then he heard a hiss, and the air began to smell odd before Scott's whole world went dark.

COMPOUNDED TROUBLE

Ross watched helplessly as Scott ran out of the restaurant. He was about to run after him when Stan caught his attention. "Let him be. No need to wear yourself out over him. I told you that you should have left him chained to your bed."

Glaring at the man, Ross had enough. "Fuck you Stan. I was *finally* getting him to learn how to be calm and you had to keep poking and prodding at him. You know Scott's been diagnosed with a panic disorder, *you asshole*. He probably ran because he was afraid of what I'll do for his outburst, but you're the one I wish I could discipline."

"That is uncalled for," Stan huffed in annoyance. "As your elder, I am entirely in my rights to provide guidance and advice regarding your duties as a bonded soulmate."

"You may have that right, but I was very clear that I did not wish for you to continue. Now, he has run off to who-knows-where. I have nothing more to say to you."

Making his way to the bar, Ross ordered a drink and tried to call Scott. In typical fashion, he wasn't answering. Ross waited with the hope that Scott would come back. When it seemed clear that he wouldn't, he settled his bill and made his way back to the hotel.

Once he was back to their room, Ross half-hoped that Scott would be there waiting for him. He was disappointed when he found it empty. *Fuck.*

Not knowing what else to do, Ross went to bed, hoping Scott would be back by morning. When morning came with no Scott in sight and no messages or calls on his phone, Ross began to worry. He called around to local hospitals and the police, but there had been no sign of him. *Now what do I do?*

That's when his phone rang. Relief flooded through him as he took the call, not even looking at the caller ID.

"Scott?! Where are you?"

"*Hey, Ross, old buddy,*" came Stuart's oily voice over the line.

Immediately Ross feared the worst.

"What have you done with him?"

"*Figured it out that fast? Well, no point in denying it. After that stunt you pulled, you forced my hand. I've now escalated the game. Give me that land, or I start sending your soulmate back to you in pieces. I think his cock and balls might be the first to go. Nullification is one of my favorite forms of punishment for unruly subs.*"

"Don't you lay a finger on him!"

"*Oh, I may do more than that. He is a pretty one, isn't he?*"

Ross felt his anger rise at the implication. "Stuart, don't you dare! We're bonded. You know what that would do to him!"

"*Then give me what I want. You have twenty-four hours, starting now.*"

The call cut off and Ross was left staring down at his phone. Growling in anger, he threw the phone across the room. A picture formed in his mind's eye of Scott, cowering in the corner of some abandoned building somewhere, terrified out of his mind.

That's when Ross remembered something. The GPS tracker that he'd asked their doctor to embed into Scott. They had been in a rush to get everything done before leaving, and he'd completely forgotten about it until now. Looking at the back of his left hand, he stroked his soulmark gently. *Hang in there, sweetheart.*

Grabbing his phone, he opened the app connected to the tracker and breathed a sigh of relief. It was still active, which meant that Stuart's people hadn't detected it. Wanting to keep this out of the news, Ross called some of his local contacts and made plans to extricate Scott before the twenty-four hours was up.

✳ ✳ ✳

Ross insisted on being there when they rescued Scott, although he was asked to hang back for his own safety. The team his contacts had put together wanted to avoid a fire fight if possible, but there was no guarantee. The important thing was for them to neutralize the kidnappers before they could harm Scott.

He immediately knew something was wrong when they came back out only a few moments later, without a single shot being fired and no sign of Scott. "You better come see this."

Following them back inside, he saw that the warehouse was empty and appeared to have been long abandoned. In the center stood a small folding card table with a box on it. It was addressed to Ross.

Opening it, he found the blood-covered GPS tracker and a note.

Nice try. Remember if you want him back intact, give me that property. – Stuart

Looking at the head of the extrication team, he asked. "Michael, is there anything else we can do? Do you have an idea who is working with Stuart and where they could be holding Scott?"

Michael shook his head. "There are a lot of options. Let me reach out to some people and see if they've heard any chatter. Maybe someone saw or heard something."

"Okay, thanks. I'll start working with my people to put together the paperwork in case I have no choice but to give in to his demands."

"That would be a shame," Michael said.

"I may not have a choice," Ross replied with a sigh as he ran his hands through his hair.

Michael patted him on the back. "We'll try to find him for you. Hang tight. I'll have someone drive you back to your hotel."

"Thanks."

∗ ∗ ∗

Ross spent the rest of the day on the phone, working with his lawyer to draw up the necessary contracts that would transfer the ownership over the Johnstown neighborhood to Stuart, *just in case.* He also talked at length with his PR director to discuss a way to minimize the fallout of this move.

Once that was done, he decided to call Dr. Landry as well. He explained the situation before asking. "So, how might this affect his panic disorder? What do I need to be aware of when I get him back?"

"*That greatly depends on how his kidnappers are treating him. If he's being reasonably cared for, given food, water, and adequate rest, then he may come out of this unscathed. On the other hand, if they use any threats, psychological abuse, or physical torture, it could make his disorder far worse. His mind isn't fragile, but even a strong one will eventually break,*" Dr. Landry explained. "*Also, I need not remind you of what might happen if Stuart carries out his threat and rapes Scott.*"

"I know ... I know," Ross replied. "Could I use that to void the contract? He promised to return Scott intact. If his mind isn't, wouldn't that void his agreement?"

"*You would need to ask your lawyer, but in my opinion, if they break his mind, then they will not be returning him intact,*" Dr. Landry confirmed.

"Thanks. That's not much consolation, but I'll make use of it if I need to. I'll make sure to add a clause to that effect into the final contract. Regardless, as soon as he's been released, I'm coming home immediately and canceling the rest of the press tour. I'd like you to come and evaluate him as soon as we're back."

"*Of course. I'll be standing by.*"

Time was running out. Ross hadn't slept since he'd woken up and taken the call from Stuart. There were only four hours left to either find Scott or hand over that property. As much as he knew he would regret this decision, he couldn't bring himself to risk Scott coming to harm.

Stuart's threats held some real consequences. The threat of nullification aside, if the man raped Scott, it would do irreparable harm. Everyone knew that once someone was fully bonded with their soulmate, they generally lost all sexual interest in others. If they foolishly had sex with someone who wasn't their soulmate, it would disrupt the chemical balance of their bond and cause a cascade of problems that often led to a complete mental breakdown. If a bonded soulmate was raped, the imbalance would be even worse, and those victims would often wind up in a catatonic state for the rest of their lives.

There was no way he could live with himself if he allowed that to happen to the man he loved, and at this point, Ross was madly in love with Scott. Sure, they were soulmates, destined to be together since birth. It ensured they were compatible, but it didn't guarantee *love at first sight*, no matter how much that romanticized notion was touted in their society. He had accepted that Scott hadn't fallen for him immediately. Scott was probably still struggling with feeling romantic affection for a man. Regardless, Ross was in love and couldn't imagine letting anything happen to Scott. The thought of losing his soulmate terrified him.

There had been some discussion about going to the public with this dilemma, shaming Stuart for daring to threaten a sacred same-sex pairing. However, Ross worried that it could backfire and lead to Scott being killed or worse. Stuart had threatened his soulmate with *nullification and rape*. The thought made Ross ill.

When the phone rang, Ross startled. "Hello?"

"Hey, Mr. Milgrave. I wanted to update you. We thought we had a lead on where Scott was being held. We just stormed the place, but he wasn't here. We're pretty sure the guys we caught inside know where

he is though. I'll let you know when we know more," Michael informed him.

A feeling of hope bloomed in Ross' chest. "Thank you for the update. I appreciate it. Please, call me the minute you know anything."

Feeling reinvigorated, Ross ordered a pot of coffee from room service. He didn't have time to rest, but he needed something to help keep him going until Scott was safely back in his arms. *I swear, I should have added a collar and leash to our contract*, he joked to himself.

After the coffee arrived, he downed a cup before taking a quick shower as well. Feeling refreshed, but without anything to do, he began to pace. There were now only three hours left to meet Stuart's demands. His feeling of hope was slowly turning to anxiousness once again, and he wished he were out there with Michael and the rest of the team looking for Scott. Now that he had all his back-up contingencies in place, the waiting around became maddening.

An unexpected knock came to his door. He hadn't ordered more room service. Going to the door, he looked through the peephole and all he saw was the top of someone's head. A sandy blond head. "Scott?!"

Opening the door, there was Scott, slumped against the doorframe. Ross caught him as he fell into the room, leaving a smear of blood on the door frame.

"Scott!" Ross cried out in alarm.

OUT OF THE FRYING PAN

Scott slowly came to and looked around. His head was throbbing, and he was lying on a dirty mattress. The walls and floor were all concrete, and the door looked like it was made of solid steel. *Fuck, where the hell am I?*

The last thing he remembered was the car he'd called to bring him back to the restaurant and then blacking out from some sort of gas in the back seat. *Have I been kidnapped? Why would anyone want me?*

Getting up, he tried to open the door. Unsurprisingly, it was locked. He pounded on it for a moment. "Hey! Is anyone out there? What do you want from me?"

When no response came, he backed away from the door and looked around the room. There were no windows, only the dirty mattress he had been lying on and the harsh light of a fluorescent lamp overhead. He paced for a while but wearing himself out was fruitless, so he slumped back onto the mattress.

This is what I get for running off like a fool, again. He imagined Ross making him wear a leash and collar from now on, which made him chuckle. Then he remembered the GPS tracker that had been embedded in the center of his back. It was in a hard-to-reach place, but he tried anyway. Reaching behind his neck and slipping his fingers under the collar of his shirt, Scott was horrified when he felt a sharp pain in his back and his fingertips brushed the edge of a bandage. The kidnappers must have found the tracker and removed it. *Fuck, I really am in deep shit.*

It felt like hours later when he heard a key opening the lock and the squeal of metal as the door was opened. Two large men came in and grabbed him, one on each arm. "The boss wants to talk to you."

They dragged him to a table holding a laptop and pushed him down into the folding chair placed in front of it. On the laptop screen was a guy with a scowl on his face. He had gray hair, dark stubble, and cruel gray eyes.

"*Well, well, well. Aren't you pretty? Figures that Ross would have such an attractive soulmate.*"

"You know Ross? What do you want with me?"

"*Ah, well, what I want is something Ross seems unwilling to part with. So, I decided to take and hold you as leverage until he gives me what I want. If not ... well let's say you are the one who will have to suffer the consequences of your soulmate's actions.*"

Scott's heart began to race. "What consequences?"

A smirk played over the man's lips. "*If Ross doesn't play ball, I promised I'd ship you back to him, piece-by-piece. Starting with your cock. Do you think he'd want you back without that pretty dick between your legs? Well, I suppose if he's on top, it won't matter. He can still use your holes. That's all you're probably good for, anyway.*"

Curling into himself at what the man described, he had to ask. "Why are you telling me all this?"

"*Oh, I love to play with my prey, not unlike a cat plays with a mouse. Plus, I wanted to get a look at that pretty face of yours. Maybe after your cock and balls, your nose might be the next to go ... or maybe one of your ears? Hmm, so many options.*"

"You're insane!"

"*Yes, I suppose I am. However, I will have my way, one way or another,*" he said with a meaningful grin before shifting his focus to the man holding Scott in the chair. "*Take him back to his cell. We'll see how long it takes for his beloved soulmate to decide to do the right thing, hmm?*"

Scott was hauled out of the chair and dragged back toward the cell he was being kept in. Everything the man ... *Stuart?* ... had said hit him like a brick wall and he went into a full panic attack. As he struggled to breathe, the guards paused. When he felt their grip loosen, he wrenched himself free and ran. He had no idea where he was going, running blindly away from his captors.

The men were yelling at him to stop, but he was in too much of a panic to pay them any heed. Scott heard a loud bang followed by a searing pain that bloomed on his right shoulder, but he kept going. Seeing a set of stairs, he ran toward them. Following the stairs, the men shouted and ran after him. Several more shots rang out, but they all missed.

Once he was on the ground floor, Scott spotted an exit sign and barreled out of the building, onto a deserted looking roadway. He looked around and saw the skyline of a city and decided to run in that direction. Taking off, he kept running, ducking into some nearby woods, dodging around trees, and leaping over logs. He didn't stop until he was out of breath and the pain in his shoulder became too much to ignore.

Collapsing to his knees, he slowly came back to his senses. Scott reached over his shoulder to where the pain was radiating, and his hand came away soaked in blood. *Fuck. I've been shot.*

Feeling around in his pockets, he looked for his cell phone and then remembered that the kidnappers must have taken it. *I need to make it back to Ross. He needs to know I got away.*

That thought kept him going as he stumbled back onto his feet and kept moving forward, albeit at a slower pace than before. He hoped he was still going in the right direction and that maybe he'd find a road where he could hitch a ride back into the city.

The sun was starting to go down when he found a paved road with a moderate number of cars driving along, He stopped to rest against a barrier and tried to hitchhike a ride. It was fully dark before someone took pity on him and stopped. The truck window lowered and an older man inside asked. "Where you headed, son?"

"I need to get back into the city. Downtown, preferably. I'm staying at the Four Towers Hotel."

"What are you doing all the way out here then? Never mind, forget I asked. I'm headed in that general direction. Hop in."

"Thank you," Scott said gratefully.

Wincing as he climbed into the truck, he tried his best to hide his injury. Hospitals could wait, he wanted to get back to Ross first.

"So, what are you in town for?"

"My soulmate, he had some business to attend to. He has some clients here he needed to meet with."

"He? Wait aren't you that fella that runs away from his soulmate because of some kind of ... panic something-or-other?"

"Panic disorder. Yeah, that's me. Please, help me get back to him. I lost my phone, and he needs to know I'm okay."

"You should be more grateful, having a soulmate like him."

Hanging his head in shame he nodded. "I know. I ... I am. He's been nothing but kind and understanding. I don't deserve him."

"That's not up to you. Fate decided that you two belong together. That you needed each other. If you keep second guessing fate, it's going to lead to trouble."

Pressing his injured shoulder tighter against the door, he couldn't agree more. "I'm in a world of trouble right now as it is."

The man chuckled knowingly. "You probably won't be able to sit for a week, once he's done with you."

* * *

The man drove him all the way to the hotel. Scott thanked him profusely before stumbling out of the truck and waving as the man drove off. Trying to stand straight, Scott made his way to the elevator and up to the top floor where their suite was. They were booked in one of the four tower suites that boasted spectacular views. Not that Scott had been able to appreciate it since they arrived.

Once in the elevator, he slumped against a wall. His body was starting to shake, and he knew he was in trouble when his legs almost gave out on him. When the elevator stopped, he stumbled out, leaning against the wall and trying desperately to make it to their room before collapsing.

When he'd made it, he realized he didn't have a key to the room. He hoped Ross was inside when he began pounding on the door. He slumped forward, leaning his head against it while he waited.

Hearing a muffled "Scott?!" from the other side of the door flooded him with relief. The door opened, and he could no longer hold himself upright, as he fell forward into Ross' arms.

* * *

When Scott woke again, the first thing he saw were fluorescent lights in the ceiling. Panic rose in his chest, and something nearby beeped faster. His throat began to constrict, as he struggled to breathe.

"Scott? Hey, it's okay. You're safe."

Looking over at whoever was talking to him, it took him a moment to refocus his eyes. "Ross?!" he croaked, barely able to speak.

"Yes, sweetheart. It's me. You're safe now. You're in the hospital. They said you were shot. You lost a lot of blood, but it missed your organs. You're going to be fine."

Scott tried to speak but his mouth was so dry. After a few attempts he managed to get out. "Thirsty ... water?"

Ross grabbed a pitcher and a plastic cup with a straw. "Sorry, here you go. Do you want to sit up a bit higher?"

Scott nodded, and Ross pressed a button that raised him up, so he was sitting upright. Taking the offered cup, he sucked at the straw, enjoying the cool water as it ran over his tongue and down his throat.

"Thanks, my mouth felt like it was stuffed with cotton," Scott said. "How long was I out, Sir?"

"It's been almost a day since I brought you in. You were in surgery, and it's taken you a while to come out of sedation."

A woman wearing a white lab coat came in. "I see our patient is awake. How are you feeling Mr. Hansen?"

"A little groggy."

"That's perfectly normal. I have you on a morphine drip for pain. I'd like to check your vitals, if you don't mind?"

Ross moved back, and she checked him over. "You were very lucky. Another inch over and that bullet would have punctured your lung. I want to keep you here for one more night, and then you will need to take it easy for a while, okay?"

"Don't worry," Ross reassured her. "We'll fly home on my private jet, and he'll get the best private nursing care that money can buy."

"What about the rest of the press tour?" Scott asked.

"I already canceled it," Ross replied. "I also have assigned a security detail to this room. No one is going to get their hands on you ever again. Especially not Stuart Grant."

"So, you know?"

"Yeah, he tried to bargain you for that property. I was ready to give it to him, too. I couldn't bear to risk your life."

"But all those people...?"

"They are safe because you managed to get away. We'll talk more about it later. Right now, you need your rest. Right, Doc?"

"Yes, absolutely. Your vitals are stable. If they remain so until tomorrow morning, I'll release you to your soulmate's care," the doctor replied.

"Thank you," Scott said.

Once the doctor left, Ross came closer and took his hand. "Now I know why the team that went to rescue you couldn't find you. We're going to have a serious discussion when we get home about that."

"You sent a team out to rescue me?"

"Of course, sweetheart. Do you think I wanted to let that monster do anything to you? If they couldn't find you in time, I would have handed over the property. There was no way I was going to let Stuart do ... *that* ... to you."

Recalling the threats made to him, Scott shuddered. "Thank you, Sir. I guess, in this instance, my panic disorder came in handy. It gave me the determination to escape and get away from my captors."

"I figured as much," Ross said as he ran his fingers through Scott's hair, ruffling it. "We'll talk about all that later. You get some rest. I'll be here when you wake up again."

"Yes, Sir."

NEGLECTED

Ross was grateful that Scott was going to be okay. It was a miracle that he had escaped and made it back to the hotel before Stuart's deadline. Unfortunately, they had to worry about what Stuart might try next. So far, they had been lucky in thwarting the man, but who knows what lengths he might take to get his way. After his latest stunt, Ross knew that he would go to any lengths to get his hands on the Johnstown neighborhood property.

If he had concrete evidence that Stuart was behind all this, Ross could bring it to the police. Unfortunately, he only had their word against Stuart's. Ross had done some checking and all the calls had come from burner phones with no connection to Stuart. For now, the only thing Ross could think to do was to step up his timeline for developing the property that Stuart wanted so desperately.

Once they were back home, he was going to rearrange his schedule and make that project a priority. It would mean having to make more compromises, to get the citizens of Johnstown on board with the project sooner, but it would be worth it. Once the area was redeveloped, he hoped the property would no longer have any appeal to Stuart.

Stuart was good at always getting his way and never getting his hands dirty. None of the things he orchestrated could ever be tied back to him. These recent failures would have him looking for other opportunities to seek revenge. Ross needed to increase the security at his estate and office building, but that wouldn't be enough.

Looking over at where Scott slept, he looked so peaceful. He was stretched out on one of the convertible loungers that Ross had outfitted in his jet. Right now, all he wanted to do was get home and take care of his soulmate. Ross was so relieved that Scott was okay and that he'd managed to escape nearly unscathed. All that mattered to him was that Scott was alive.

Picking up his phone, he called a friend of his. Someone who was very good at finding vulnerabilities and ways to exploit them. "Hey, George. I need to ask you for a favor. One that I'll pay handsomely for, of course. Find all the chinks in Stuart Grant's armor for me, please. This is a top priority. Thanks, George." That done, Ross reclined in his own seat and tried to get some sleep for the rest of their flight.

* * *

Once they were back home, Ross made sure Scott was settled in and updated the staff on what happened. He was going to make sure Scott took it easy and had his every need taken care of. He then called in his private physician and Dr. Landry to come and check on Scott as well.

That evening, Ross brought their dinner up to the bedroom on a tray, along with the medication that Scott had been prescribed. "Hey Scott, how are you feeling?"

"Wow, I've heard of breakfast in bed, but never dinner," Scott teased. "The pain meds your doctor put me on have me feeling pretty good."

"That's good. I have your next dose here. Just remember, no matter how good you feel, you need to take it easy for a while, okay?" Ross reminded him as he set the tray on the bed and settled in next to Scott.

"Yes, Sir."

Since Scott's dominant arm was still in a sling, Ross insisted on feeding Scott and making sure he took his medication.

"I should tell you, starting tomorrow, I'm going to be spending more time at the office," Ross informed him as he fed Scott another bite. "I need to get a step ahead of Stuart before all hell breaks loose. We've upset his plans twice now, and he's going to be out for blood. I fear what he might try next and things could get ugly."

"Wha' am I s'posed to do if you're gone all day?" Scott slurred, as his medication kicked in.

"I could bring you your laptop, and you could work on that next novel. I know your publisher is being hard on you right now but give it some time. Maybe by the time you're done, your readers will be ready to give you another chance?"

"'Kay," Scott agreed sleepily. "I'd like t'work on that. I've got lots of ideas."

"That's perfect. I'm sorry that I can't work from home, but I need the resources I have at the office if I'm going to pull this off," Ross said as he got up and set the tray aside. "Do you need anything else?"

"Jus' you, Sir."

Ross smirked. "Okay, hang in there. I'll join you shortly."

After Ross readied himself for bed and slipped under the covers, Scott yawned and asked sleepily. "How long d'ya think it'll take?"

Ross shrugged. "I'm not sure. At least a week, maybe more."

"Hmm, 'kay," Scott replied before his head sank onto Ross' shoulder, sound asleep.

* * *

Over the next week, Ross spent most of his time at the office. He and his team had accelerated their timeline for the Johnstown redevelopment project, and Ross insisted on being hands on. It was crucial that everything went smoothly. Ross spent twelve to sixteen-hour days at the office, crashing at his downtown suite almost every night.

During the first few days of this grueling schedule, the one occasion when Ross made it back to the estate, Scott wasn't in their bed. Ross immediately feared that Scott had run off again. He checked the security footage and saw that Scott had gone to sleep in his private suite. It was late, so Ross decided not to disturb him.

The next morning, he checked in with his security personnel to make sure they were keeping Scott safe and under surveillance. "Yeah, he's not happy about it, but he's been staying put," reassured Daryl, the head of his security team. "He's cussed us out a few times when we wouldn't let him leave the house."

Ross chuckled, picturing a frustrated Scott. "If it happens again, let me know," Ross said. "I'll set him straight."

"Yes, sir!"

"Thanks, Daryl."

Finally, over a week later, all the plans for Johnstown had been finalized, and the groundbreaking had been scheduled. Once the last meeting wrapped up, Ross went back to his office to check on his messages. There was one from George, the investigator he called to dig into Stuart's past. Picking up his phone, he immediately called George back.

"George! It's Ross. I just got your message. You said you have something for me?"

"*Yeah, it took a lot of digging but I came up with some really good dirt on that guy,*" George said. "*I had all my reports messengered to you a couple of hours ago, they should be on your desk.*"

Looking over his desk, Ross spotted the packet. "I found it. Thank you so much, George. Send my assistant the bill and I'll make sure it gets paid right away."

"*Pleasure doing business with you, Ross, as always.*"

Remembering a discussion he'd had with Scott some time ago, Ross stopped George from hanging up. "Hang on George. There's something else I need your help on."

Once Ross filled George in on the details, he hung up and sat down. Opening the packet, he read through the reports. *This should be more than enough to damn Stuart to hell and back*, Ross thought with a self-satisfied smile.

To celebrate, Ross decided to come home early and surprise Scott. He bought a bouquet of red roses and a bottle of champagne, hoping to tear Scott away from his book long enough to have a fun evening together.

When he got home, he went to Scott's suite where he'd been holing himself up. The door was locked, which wasn't unusual.

When he knocked, no one came to the door. "Hey, Scott, I know you're in there. Please, take a break and let me in?"

Waiting for a full minute with no response, Ross fished the keys out of his pocket. There was no room in his estate that he didn't have access to. He hated to violate Scott's privacy like this, but he worried about him when he would shut down and not respond.

Once he had the door open, Ross looked through the suite, finding Scott curled up in the bedroom on his old bed. His shoulders were wracked with silent sobs. "Hey, Scott," Ross said gently as he lay the roses and champagne down and sat on the bed. "What's wrong, sweetheart?"

Scott shot up and glared at him, his eyes red and puffy. "What's wrong?! Are you fucking kidding me? You practically abandon me for *weeks*, while keeping me a virtual prisoner at *your* estate, and you dare ask me what's wrong? Some soulmate you are!"

Ross reeled back from the verbal onslaught, completely floored by the accusations. "Hey, where the hell is this coming from? You know why I've had to spend so much time at the office the past couple of weeks, and you're hardly a prisoner."

For a moment Scott stared, trying to control his breathing. "No, I don't fucking know why you chose to abandon me after we came back. You never said one word. You were just gone! After you promised not to abandon me like my dad did ... what the hell was I supposed to think?"

Shooting up from the bed, Ross felt a surge of frustration. "What do you mean I never said anything? Don't you remember?! On that night, after we got back home, I brought dinner up, and I told you I had to spend more time at the office.

I had to get ahead of Stuart and whatever he was planning next."

Sitting up, Scott wiped his face on his sleeve and glared daggers at him. "No, I don't fucking remember that! I was hopped up on pain killers, remember? Everything from around that time is really fuzzy."

"Shit, you're right," Ross conceded, pacing back and forth for a moment. Taking a deep breath, Ross settled himself back on the bed and rubbed his face. "I'm sorry, sweetheart. I should have realized how out of it you were."

"Damn right you should have," Scott groused, folding his arms across his chest. "Why the hell did you add all that stuff into our contract about communication, when you clearly suck at it?"

"Fair enough, I deserve that," Ross said with a sigh before a thought occurred to him. "However, you could have picked up your phone and called, if it was bothering you that much."

All the tension in Scott drained out of him as his face fell at that realization. "Ugh!" Scott uttered as he hid his face in his hands.

Reaching out, Ross gently touched Scott's shoulder. "Hey, let's have dinner? We can talk more, and I can explain why I've been so busy."

Scott looked up and stared at him for a moment before nodding. "Okay." Then his eyes flicked over to the roses and champagne. "Are those...?"

Picking them up he handed them to Scott. "Yeah, I came home early to celebrate and give you the good news. I ... well let's talk over dinner, okay?"

Scott put the flowers and bottle aside and nodded. Then he crawled over, grabbing a hold of Ross and clung to him. "Please, just hold me first," Scott pleaded. "I missed you so much."

Wrapping his arms around Scott, Ross hugged him tightly. "I'm sorry. I shouldn't have left you alone so long and I should have kept you in the loop."

Nodding into his shoulder, Scott agreed. "Yeah."

Stroking his hair, Ross kissed Scott's head. "I'll make it up to you, I promise. Let's go have dinner first, okay? I called ahead and it should be ready."

Sitting up, Scott wiped his face and nodded again. "Okay. I am pretty hungry."

* * *

They both went to freshen up and met in the dining room, already set for dinner. Once their food was served, Ross started to explain. "After Stuart took you ... I was beside myself. When you made it back to me, I swore to keep him from trying something else. I needed to keep you safe, which is why I told my security guards not to let you leave the estate unattended. I'm sorry you felt like you were being kept a prisoner. I don't want to lose you. Not again."

Scott sighed and looked into his eyes, studying them for a moment. "Yeah, okay. I don't want to fall back into that man's clutches again, but I was going stir crazy."

"I'm sorry about that. I'll work something out. I hope you're okay with at least having a bodyguard accompany you in the future?"

"Yeah, that would be okay," Scott conceded.

"Good," Ross said. "Now, as to what I've been working on. I knew I had to accelerate the timeline on the redevelopment project in Johnstown. We're ready to break ground on the Milgrave-Hansen Redevelopment Project. I'm finally getting to see my dream come true of revitalizing my old neighborhood."

Looking somewhat surprised, Scott blinked for a moment. "Milgrave-Hansen? You included my name on the project?"

Smiling Ross nodded. "Yeah, I did. The project isn't just for me anymore. It's for both of us."

"I ... I don't know what to say," Scott stammered, speechless.

Reaching out to take Scott's hand, Ross confessed. "You're the most important thing in my life. I am sorry you felt neglected the past couple of weeks, but everything I've been doing has been with you in mind."

Emotion began to well in Scott's eyes, so Ross pulled his hand closer and kissed it with a smile, before changing the topic. "Besides working on that project, I also hired an investigator to find some of Stuart's vulnerabilities. I hoped to find something I could exploit. I need to be able to beat him at his own game."

"Wow, did they find any?"

"They found a few. I wanted to discuss them with you first before going after him. I don't want to do anything that will compromise my ethics, but there are a few possibilities that would send him a strong message to leave us alone."

Looking down, Scott looked like he was trying to retain his composure. "So, you *really* weren't staying away from me, because you couldn't stand the sight of me anymore?" Scott asked, almost to himself before looking up at Ross with tears in his eyes. "I was convinced that after running away from you again that ... that you didn't want me anymore."

Squeezing Scott's hand, Ross tried to reassure him. "Oh, Scott, sweetheart no! I'm sorry you felt like that. I knew you needed time to heal from the gunshot, so I dove headfirst into my work. I'm sorry. I should have been keeping you apprised of what was going on."

"I feel like an ass. You were right. I should have called."

"Well, it's partially my fault that I didn't stay in touch and keep you updated either. I get so wrapped up with work sometimes, I forget the rest of the world exists. What can I do to make it up to you?"

"Well, it's been a while ... I've missed my Sir."

"You have? Have you been my good boy or my naughty boy?" Ross asked with a wicked grin.

Scott shrugged and then looked up at him shyly. "A little of both?"

"That's exactly what I wanted to hear. How about we take this to the bedroom?"

Scott downed the rest of his drink and nodded. "Yes, Sir."

Leading the way, Ross was eager to get his hands on Scott after so long. Once they were in the master suite, Ross locked the door behind them. "Are you all healed up?"

Nodding Scott removed the t-shirt he was wearing. The scarred skin where the bullet had violated his body was still shiny and pink, but it was clearly healed.

Tracing the scar with his fingers made Ross shiver. He leaned over and captured Scott's mouth with his. It had been far too long since they'd been intimate. Ross decided then he needed to rectify that and never let so much time pass again.

"So, tell me ... how were you naughty and how were you good?"

"I was naughty when I ran away from you at your business dinner. I deserve to be punished for disobeying and not talking to you before I ran off. That left me vulnerable and gave Stuart a chance to grab me," Scott admitted. "However, I was good because I escaped from those men and came straight back to you. All I could think about was making it back, so you knew I was okay."

"Oh, my good, sweet boy. Thank you for your confession. I never did punish you for that, did I? Do you need me to punish you? Do you need absolution?"

"Yes, Sir. Please."

"Undress for me sweetheart, and bend over the end of the bed, with your feet on the floor."

Scott eagerly obeyed, and a few moments later Ross was admiring the beautiful curve of Scott's ass as he presented it for punishment.

Taking off his suit jacket and tie, before rolling up his sleeves, Ross contemplated the best punishment he could administer here, outside of his playroom. A wicked grin crossed his face as he undid the buckle of his belt. "For such an infraction, especially one that led to so much trouble, requires a suitably harsh punishment, don't you agree?"

"Yes, Sir!" Scott replied eagerly, his body practically vibrating with anticipation.

Making sure the hiss of the leather coming loose from his belt loops was clearly heard, Ross then doubled the belt in his hand and snapped it a couple of times for effect.

"You will take fifty from my belt. Count them and apologize after each lick. Is that understood?"

A delicious shudder ran through Scott's body as he processed that. "Yes, Sir."

"What's your color?"

"Green, Sir. Very green."

Stripe after stripe landed on Scott's backside, turning his ass and upper thighs a dark crimson. By the time the last lash landed, he was practically screaming out the count. "Fifty! I'm sorry! I'm so sorry, Sir."

Ross put aside the belt. "You're forgiven now, Scott, but I'm not done with you yet. I want to take you, right where you are, while your ass is still hot and throbbing.

Going into the bedside table to grab their bottle of lube, he had a thought. "Have you been playing with yourself in the weeks I've neglected you?"

"Yes, Sir. I have Sir," Scott confessed.

"Hmm, *very naughty*. I may need to consider putting you in chastity for that," Ross teased as he spread apart Scott's cheeks and poured lube on his hole. "I'm going to open you up with my cock. I want you to still feel me all day tomorrow and not forget who owns this beautiful ass of yours."

"You do, Sir. I'm sorry I thought you forgot about me. Please, I need you to remind me that I belong to you, Sir."

Ross didn't bother undressing. He merely unzipped and pulled out his raging erection, slicking himself with more lube. "Are you ready for me to fill you up, sweetheart?"

"Yes, Sir. *Please*, Sir!"

Grabbing Scott's hip, Ross lined himself up and began rocking in and out of his hole, slowly opening him up. As he sank deeper, making a space for himself deep inside of Scott, he relished the hot, velvety tightness. He knew that Ross' hole must be burning from the intrusion, but he was still moaning in ecstasy.

A few more thrusts and Ross slid home, buried to the hilt. Pausing, he bent over to pepper kisses across Scott's back. "You're so good and you take me so well. Your ass always fits me so perfectly."

"My ass missed you … I … I missed you so much, Sir," Scott said with a whimper.

"I know, I'm sorry, sweetheart. From now on, I'm going to make sure I remind you every day that you're mine."

Ross began to fuck Scott with a slow drag out and a fast snap back in, driving his hips hard against Scott's well-punished ass. Moaning and whimpering under the onslaught, Scott was completely pliant as Ross continued to pound into him, chasing his own pleasure.

So lost in his own ecstasy, he almost didn't pick up Scott's pleas. "Please, Sir. Please…"

Slowing down his thrusts, Ross bent closer to Scott's ear. "Please what, sweetheart? What do you need?"

"Let me see you, Sir? Please?"

Sliding himself out, he stepped back. "You asked me so nicely, how can I deny such a request? Go on, get on your back for me."

Scott turned, laying on his back and wincing as his ass touched the bed. He spread his legs wide, inviting Ross. Pulling Scott so his ass hung off the edge of the bed, he plunged back in, causing his lover to cry out. "Is this what you wanted?"

Looking up at him, Scott nodded. "Yeah. I needed to know it's you that's giving me what I need. Taking your pleasure from me. I need you so much, Sir."

A well of emotion bloomed in Ross' chest at Scott's words. Leaning down, he kissed him deeply, parting his lips, caressing his mouth with his tongue, while languidly sliding his cock in and out. "I need you too, Scott. So much. Sorry I neglected you for so long."

Wrapping his arms around Scott, he fucked him slow and steady, whispering promises and endearments into his ear. Scott moaned and writhed beneath him, gasping anytime his prostate was grazed. From the shift in tone of his whimpers, he could tell Scott was getting close. "Are you going to come for me, sweetheart?"

"I'm so close, Sir. Please? May I?"

"Yes, of course. Come, sweetheart. Come for me."

Moving his hips faster, rutting into Scott as he felt him clench around his cock, until he arched under him and screamed his release. Scott's come splashed hot and sticky between them, and Ross couldn't hold back anymore. Moving upright, he chased his own release, pounding into Scott hard and fast.

The tension in his groin built until he roared when he came. He shot spurt after spurt of his seed deep into Scott, holding himself still as his cock pulsed.

After the peak of pleasure had passed, he looked down to see Scott smiling at him with adoration. "You're gorgeous when you come, Sir."

"I could say the same about you. Now, stay put for a moment. I'll be right back."

Going into the bathroom he wetted a washcloth and brought a towel to clean them both up. "I want to cuddle, but how about we throw some sweats on and cuddle on the couch in front of the fireplace?"

QUALITY TIME

Scott happily settled into Ross' arms on the couch, in front of a crackling fire. After so many weeks apart, it was good to have his soulmate back. Feeling a little foolish for having assumed that Ross abandoned him, he still smiled as he felt Ross kiss the top of his head. "So, tell me about your new novel," Ross said. "I haven't taken enough interest in your writing. Have you finished it?"

"Not yet, but I made a lot of progress while you were busy. At least when I wasn't moping around, thinking you didn't want me anymore," Scott replied with a chuckle. "Since your security guards wouldn't let me off the grounds, I had nothing else better to do. This was the most productive I've been with my writing in a long while. My mood fueled some interesting new plot twists."

"Well, at least some good came out of my neglectfulness!" Ross teased. "How soon until you finish it? Do you need help finding an editor?"

Scott shook his head. "It'll take me at least a couple more weeks to finish writing it. My publisher reached out and they are harassing me to finish it, so they'll provide the editing again."

"I thought you said your publisher wasn't interested in your next novel because of dropping sales?"

"That was before our radio interview. I guess that renewed interest in my books again. I'm glad they reached out and have been pushing me to produce a new book. If they hadn't, I would have been beside myself the last couple of weeks."

"Make me a promise? If you feel like I'm working too much and neglecting you again, come talk to me. Call my office or text me if I'm not home. Let me know, okay? We might be soulmates, but I can't read your mind. You need to communicate with me."

Turning in Ross' arms so he could look him in the eye. "Okay, but that goes for you as well. You thought you had told me what you were working on, but I was so out of it, it didn't register. If I'm not well, make sure you tell me more than once. If I had known, I wouldn't have broken down like that."

"You're right," Ross agreed. "I'll keep that in mind, especially if I know work is going to get crazy."

"Okay, thanks. This relationship stuff is hard. No wonder I never got into one before."

"Never? So, you only did weekend hookups, and that was it?"

Shrugging Scott nodded. "I figured, what's the point? If I did meet my soulmate, then any relationship I was in was null-and-void. If I didn't, well, there was always time after I hit thirty-five and wouldn't be expected to attend those parties anymore. How about you?"

"I've had a couple of serious boyfriends, but I get what you mean. They were always taken away from me after they found their soulmates. It hurt, but I understood. I had to keep hoping that I'd eventually find you," Ross said, squeezing Scott in his arms.

"You didn't realize you had to go slumming for me, huh?" Scott joked.

"Hey, don't you dare say that! Remember, I told you, I grew up poor, besides that party was hardly in the slums. I guess I focused a lot more on getting myself out of poverty when I was younger. I never paid attention to the whole soulmate thing. Sure, I went to the parties, but I always hid away in a corner, so I could keep working. If we had ever been at the same party when we were younger, we never got close enough for our marks to activate."

"I figured you and I never went to the same parties. You know, I've wanted to ask. Why were you at *that* party? The one where we met?"

"I decided a couple of years ago, after my last boyfriend found his soulmate, that it was time I took finding my own more seriously. So, instead of going back to the same small circle of parties I had been attending, I widened my scope. I had my personal assistant map out all the parties in the city and surrounding areas. She put together a plan where I would likely run across every unpartnered person in the area at least once."

"Wow, so you were serious about finding me, huh? Were you that sure I'd be at one of the local area parties?"

"No, I wasn't, but statistically soulmates have an eighty-three percent chance of being born within a one-hundred-mile radius of each other. I had to exhaust all local options first. Since I was established with my business and financially secure, I could devote more time to finding you. I was tired of always losing my partner to their soulmate. I needed *you*. Which makes me feel like a real ass for neglecting you the last couple of weeks."

Scott snorted. "So why is it *my ass* that's sore now ... *Sir?*"

Ross laughed and pulled Scott closer. "You know exactly why. Hopefully, *your ass* won't forget again?"

Before Scott could respond, Ross pulled him in for a kiss. It was soft and sensuous, lacking the heat or desperation from earlier. It conveyed more tenderness and affection than Scott had yet experienced with Ross, and it brought up a well of emotion inside of him. He clung to Ross as tears slid unbidden down his cheeks.

Breaking the kiss, Ross looked at him with wonder, as he cupped his face, wiping the tears with his thumbs. "Why the tears, sweetheart? Did I say something wrong?"

Shaking his head, Scott leaned into Ross' touch. "No, I ... the way you kissed me ... it felt like you were trying to convey something ... unspoken."

Ross looked at him for a long moment before taking a breath. "I guess it has gone unspoken. I wasn't sure if you were ready to hear it after everything that's been going on."

Scott searched Ross' eyes. "Tell me?"

"I love you, Scott."

"Oh, Ross," Scott breathed. He leaned in for another kiss, while tears pricked at his eyes again.

Breaking the kiss and looking into Ross' eyes, he couldn't hold back his own confession. "Ross ... *Sir* ... I ... I love you, too. That's why the thought of you no longer ... wanting me..."

When Ross' breath hitched, Scott hurried to continue. "I realized it when I escaped from the kidnappers. All I could think about was getting back to you, letting you know I was safe. I was afraid of how worried you must have been."

Scott saw the raw emotion in Ross' eyes as his own tears welled. "Yeah, I was so worried when you didn't come back after running off, but when Stuart called me the next morning? I was terrified of what he might do to you, and how that might affect you. I've known I was in love with you even before then, but that's what cemented it for me. I was prepared to sacrifice everything, so I could get you back in one piece."

"I know, and I couldn't let you do that. I couldn't let you sacrifice your childhood home or let Stuart ruin that neighborhood. The people living there deserve better than what that monster would have done."

"That's why I added your name to the project, sweetheart. They deserve to know you had a part to play in the revitalization of their neighborhood," Ross explained.

"That still blows me away. I can't believe you did that. Will you let me go and visit the area once it's finished?"

"Yes, of course. I'm sorry you have felt trapped here. I'll admit I've been overprotective since everything that happened. Will you allow me to assign you a driver and bodyguard for whenever you want to go out? It would help me worry about you less."

"If it means I get to leave the house occasionally, then yes. Whatever it takes."

"Deal. Hey, I'm feeling a bit peckish. Why don't we go raid the kitchen for a snack?" Ross suggested.

"Yeah, that sounds good."

* * *

The next day, Ross decided to work from home. After lunch he asked Scott to join him in his study. "I mentioned yesterday that I found out a few of Stuart's vulnerabilities. I'd like to discuss them and run by you some possible ideas of how to exploit them. I'd love to get your feedback before I proceed."

"Okay. Thanks for including me. I'd like to see him taken down, so he can't hurt anyone else," Scott agreed. "What have you found?"

"The big thing that we discovered is the reason why Stuart is hell bent to get that land from me. There is a network of old tunnels under that part of the city. By all accounts, he wants to utilize them to further some illegal activity he's engaged in. By tearing down all the buildings and developing on top of those tunnels, he would have a way to run all sorts of contraband into the city directly from the docks."

"Wow, can you prove it?"

"I think so. My contact managed to get his hands on some of his plans as well as verified the existence of those tunnels himself. They aren't on any plans at City Hall either, so they've either been forgotten, or the existence of them has been erased from the records for some reason."

"So, what do you plan to do with the information?"

"I have to consider that carefully. If I hand it over to the police, it would ruin his entire business. Clearly, a lot of what he does is unethical and illegal, but thousands of people could be out of a job. It would also destroy his family, many of whom are good people, despite Stuart's questionable ethics."

"What else can you do?"

"Hold this information over his head and use it to get him to back off and hopefully leave us alone. I'm not sure he'll fall for it, but it's worth a shot," Ross replied. "Also, knowing about those tunnels gives me a great idea for that area. I could include them in my redevelopment project as an efficient means to bring goods into the neighborhood without increasing traffic or pollution."

"Look at you, already finding an ethical and responsible way to make the most of this situation. How did I get so lucky to have you as my soulmate?" Scott praised.

"You're as lucky as I am, sweetheart."

Looking away from Ross, Scott shook his head. "Nah, you're stuck with a fuckup for a soulmate. A fuckup who keeps running away from you when I should be grateful to be yours."

Standing up and rounding his desk, Ross pulled Scott to his feet. Using his right hand, he guided Scott's chin up, forcing him to look him in the eye. "First, it's not your fault that you suffer from a panic disorder. That doesn't make you a *fuckup*. It makes you human. Second, you're a successful author who is writing another novel. That takes passion and dedication. That is not the mark of a *fuckup*. Finally, you have exceeded my expectations with your submission to me. I would have been happy with a vanilla partner if that was my fate, but you have taken to everything so well."

Feeling the heat rise in his cheeks at the sincere praise, Scott tried to duck his head to get away from Ross' gaze.

"Now, if I hear one more word from you insulting yourself, you will be bent over and taking my belt so fast your head will spin. I love you and no one insults those that I love. Not even themselves. Understood?" Ross said firmly.

Swallowing thickly at the visual that crossed his mind's eye, Scott nodded. "Yes. Yes, Sir."

"You like that idea, don't you?" Ross asked, his hand sliding down to cup Scott's crotch.

"Um, well, maybe?" Scott admitted as his dick twitched with interest.

Leaning closer, Ross asked. "Would you like me to bend you over this desk and warm that beautiful backside of yours?" Ross purred into his ear.

Despite his ass still feeling sore from his previous night's punishment, he nodded shyly. "Yes, Sir. Please, Sir?"

"I can't deny you when you're being so polite and blushing so pretty," Ross said, his voice becoming rough with arousal. He pulled Scott in for a deep, filthy kiss, holding him possessively behind the neck, while his other hand palmed Scott's cock through his jeans.

"Pull your pants down and bend over," Ross ordered as soon as he broke the kiss.

His hands quickly moved to his fly and popped the button and lowered the zipper before he slid his jeans and boxers down to his knees. Then Scott bent himself over the cool surface of the wood. The desk was large and sturdy and could easily withstand any onslaught Ross might subject him to.

"Good boy. Since this isn't a punishment, I'm only going to warm your ass with my hand today. It's still red from yesterday, so this will hurt a bit more than it normally would. What's your color?"

"Green, Sir."

Gently, Ross placed one hand on Scott's lower back to hold him still, while his other hand massaged his still sore buttocks. "You're always so eager. You're such a perfect submissive for me. I'll gladly spank you until you realize that, my love."

A flurry of spanks began to land on his ass. They came so fast; it took a moment for Scott's mind to catch up with what was happening. The spanks stung on the surface, but they also reawakened the deeper pain from the belting he'd received the night before.

The spanks simultaneously hurt and felt good at the same time, and his cock was once again enjoying the proceedings. Between each flurry of spanks, Ross would pause and massage his cheeks. At each new round of spanks, his dick would get harder until he was leaking all over the floor.

"You're so hard," Ross remarked. "Can you come for me? Just from being spanked?"

Before Scott could even answer, another flurry of spanks rained down, and he began to spiral toward an orgasm, as his groin tightened. Scott felt like he was flying as his body relaxed and he fully submitted to the spanking.

Tension and heat coiled, and he floated on the crashing tide of ecstasy as spank after spank landed on his abused flesh. He screamed his release as Ross spanked him through it, landing a few harder blows that sent his mind reeling.

When he came back to himself, Scott's underwear and jeans were pulled back up and he was sitting dazed in one of the wingback chairs. Ross was squatting next to him and handed him a glass of water as soon as he realized Scott was coming back to himself.

"Welcome back," Ross said with a wry smile.

"Wow, how long was I out for?" Scott asked. "That was incredible. I had no idea I was capable of that."

"You didn't only come from being spanked, you slipped into subspace," Ross explained. "How do you feel?"

"Wonderful, Sir, but..."

"But I didn't fuck you. This isn't always about my personal gratification. It's also about giving you what you need. This was all about you. I can get my rocks off another time."

Letting the words sink in for a moment, he took a couple of gulps of water, realizing how dry his throat felt. Ross was still squatting next to him and he reached out and caressed his face. "I am the luckiest soulmate. I love you so much, Sir." It felt good to be able to say it, knowing the feeling was mutual.

"We're both lucky. Now drink up and let's go hit the hot tub. We can discuss my plans for Stuart and the Milgrave-Hansen Project there."

"Sounds good."

PLAYROOM

Ross tried to limit his time at the office, working from home more frequently. He also included Scott more often in his planning meetings, mostly as a silent observer. He hadn't started another novel yet, so Ross wanted to make sure Scott remained busy. His creative mind proved to be a great counterpoint to his more analytical one, and Ross found himself often bouncing ideas off Scott.

They made a great team and soon had things in motion to thwart Stuart once-and-for-all, while the Milgrave-Hansen Project kept going full-steam-ahead. The domestic discipline aspect of their relationship was also having the intended effect of centering and grounding Scott, and he hadn't had a panic incident recently. Ross had to admit he also enjoyed administering the routine maintenance spankings that he'd been neglecting to give.

They were enjoying dinner in the dining room one evening when Scott paused. "May I ask you something, Sir?"

"Yes, of course, sweetheart."

"After everything that's happened, I never had a chance to bring this up, but I've been wondering; what happened to your parents? You never mention them."

Putting his fork down, he picked up his napkin and wiped his mouth. "I was wondering when you might get around to asking. That is a rather long story, one that might take some alcohol. Suffice it to say that it was because of them, I was driven to my current line of work."

"Ah, so it's a sore subject. I'm sorry."

"No, it's okay. You have a right to know. Let's talk about it over drinks later, okay?"

"Yeah, alright."

After dinner, Ross led Scott to the living room, so they could sit together on the large couch by the fireplace. Winter had come and there was a definite chill in the air.

Ross poured them both a drink and then handed one to Scott as they both settled on the couch. "So, you already know that my family was pretty poor, and we lived in one of the row houses in Johnstown."

Scott nodded. "Yeah, you're sort of famous for being the rags-to-riches billionaire with a *heart-of-gold.*"

Snorting out a laugh Ross felt his cheeks heat. "I hate that description. I mean, yeah, I try to do the right thing whenever I can with my developments, but even I've had to play hardball and make the less ethical choice on occasion. I would never have gotten to where I am today if I hadn't."

"That sucks, but it's how the world works, isn't it?"

Taking a long pull from his drink, Ross nodded. Dredging up these memories felt like a heaviness on his chest. "So, about my parents. They were good people who were dealt a bad hand in life. Neither had found their soulmate. They were an unbonded couple, married when they were in their late 30s. He worked construction, and she was a cleaning lady."

"Sounds like they were hardworking people. So, what happened?"

"Someone bought out the construction company my dad worked for and laid everyone off. They brought in their own people. My dad looked for work elsewhere, but all the folks that had worked for the original company were blacklisted. It was some petty revenge against the former owners," Ross said with a sigh. "My dad ended up taking lots of odd jobs and my mom had to take on extra cleaning shifts to put food on the table. She worked herself into an early grave."

Reaching out and taking his hand, Scott looked at him with sympathy. "That's rough. How old were you?"

"About eight or nine. Dad took it hard. They might not have been soulmates, but he loved her. It ate at him that he was unable to provide for us. He hung on until I was about sixteen, but he slowly withered away. One night he went to bed and never woke up again. The coroner said *natural causes*, but I've always had to wonder. He was only in his fifties at the time."

"That sounds a little like what happened to my mom. She did her best to raise me, but the years of separation wore on her and in the end, it was like she gave up on life," Scott shared. "So, what happened after you lost your dad?"

"I went to stay with some relatives until I was old enough to be on my own. I still blame that company that bought out where my dad worked and blacklisted all those people," Ross explained. "I never understood why they did that. It made no sense to me and I never got an explanation. So, I was determined to get powerful enough to buy them out and fix the damage they had done to our community. They were the first big acquisition Milgrave United made."

"Could this be why we're soulmates?" Scott wondered aloud. "Like, fate knew we would both have tough childhoods, and we'd be able to relate to each other because of it?"

Ross caressed Scott's hand and let his mind wander for a moment, thinking over the many milestones and life choices he had made to get to where he was today. "Maybe so. At least we both can appreciate how important our connection to each other is. Even, if you do keep trying to run away from it," Ross teased.

"After what happened the last time I ran, I promise, I'm going to think twice before I do it again. I never want to be in the clutches of that monster again."

"Yeah, unlike me, who only wants to lock up your family jewels once in a while," Ross said with a wicked twinkle in his eye.

"Well see, *that's* kind of hot," Scott admitted sheepishly. "However, I have no desire to lose them completely."

"I was horrified when Stuart made that threat. I worried about what he might be doing to further traumatize you. I would have never let that happen."

"Yeah, I know. Thank you, and thanks for telling me about your folks ... that makes me feel even closer to you, knowing that."

Feeling his heart swell, Ross scooted closer to Scott and caressed his face before sliding his hand around to the back of his neck and pulling him in for a chaste kiss. "That means a lot to me to hear you say that, sweetheart."

"Thanks. So, is the meeting with Stuart still happening tomorrow?"

"Yes, you know it is," Ross replied, noting how Scott's form tensed. "Are you nervous about facing him again?"

"Yes, Sir," Scott replied, while ducking his head.

"Hmm, do you need some time in the playroom?"

Scott shrugged while a deep blush spread across his features. "Yeah ... um ... yes. Yes, I do, Sir."

Caressing and squeezing Scott's neck where his hand still rested, Ross kissed his temple. "Finish your drink and then go on ahead. You know what to do," Ross instructed, handing Scott the key.

"Yes, Sir!" Scott replied brightly, downing his drink before giving Ross a quick peck and heading upstairs.

Taking his time to finish his drink, Ross contemplated the scene he'd like to do with Scott. He wanted Scott to feel loved and cherished. He smiled to himself when he hit on the perfect idea. Finishing his drink, he set aside the glass and made his way up to the playroom.

Stepping into the room and locking it behind him, he was pleased to see Scott completely nude and kneeling in the center of the room. He made his way over to him, running his fingers through the man's soft hair. "I'm going to show you exactly how much I care about you. This scene is all about you and what you need tonight. Pick one implement and one piece of equipment. Explain why you are choosing each before we begin."

Watching with interest, his eyes followed Scott as he made his way to the wall where all the implements hung. Taking his time to touch and weigh several in his hands, Scott chose a leather strap.

Looking around the room at the different equipment, he made his way to the St. Andrews Cross. "I've chosen, Sir."

"Good boy. So, why did you choose this implement?" Ross asked as he took the strap from Scott's hands.

"You haven't used it on me yet, and I'm curious what being strapped feels like. The feel of the strap reminds me of your belt, but heavier and wider? I'll admit I probably like the feel of that belt more than I should, Sir," Scott said with a furious blush.

"Why the cross?"

"A combination of reasons. You haven't used it with me yet, and the idea of being spread open like that, instead of bent over a bench or horse, and forced to face the wall. I think it will make me feel vulnerable? I need that tonight ... to be at your mercy, Sir."

"Thank you for sharing the reason for your choices. Please, go strap on the leather cuffs," Ross instructed as he began to roll up his shirtsleeves.

Coming back with the cuffs secured on his ankles and wrists, Ross tested to make sure they were properly secured. "Step up to the cross, facing the wall."

Securing the cuffs to the cross left Scott completely spread-eagled, exposing the beautiful lines of his back, buttocks, and legs. "You do make a pretty picture like this," Ross praised, running his hand down Scott's spine and caressing his ass.

"Thank you, Sir."

"I'll begin with my hand, to warm your skin, and then give you a nice strapping. I won't count. Let me know when you've had enough by calling out yellow, okay sweetheart?"

"Yes, Sir. I'll call out yellow when I've had enough."

"Good boy."

Setting aside the strap, Ross caressed and massaged Scott's ass before applying the first spank. He worked up a steady rhythm, warming Scott's buttocks and upper thighs with his hand. Soon Scott was moaning and writhing as the heat built up under his skin.

Spank after spank landed, slowly pinking Scott's skin. The soft cries of pain mixed with pleasure coming from Scott were music to Ross' ears.

Once the right color of pink was achieved, Ross stepped back to admire his work. "Are you ready to feel the lick of the strap, sweetheart?" Ross asked as he picked up the implement.

"Yes, Sir," Scott replied, his body trembling with need.

Aiming for Scott's beautifully pinked ass, he laid stripe after stripe onto his heated flesh. Scott's cries were louder now, and his skin began to darken as he laid one precise blow after another, careful not to overlap them.

Once Ross had worked his way down to Scott's thighs, he checked in. "What's your color?"

"Green, Sir," Scott rasped out.

Taking a breath, Ross began again, strapping over the previous welts. Scott's cries became more anguished this time and Ross hesitated between blows until Scott whimpered. "Green. *Please*, Sir."

It wasn't until he landed a particularly hard blow to Scott's sensitive sit spot that Scott cried out. "Yellow! I'm ... yellow, Sir."

"Good boy. You had me a little worried for a moment. Take a breath."

As Scott took several deep breaths, Ross went to the room's mini-fridge and grabbed a bottle of water. He then unhooked Scott's restraints and helped him turn around, before securing him back to the cross. "Drink some water, my love."

Scott took several deep drinks from the bottle as Ross held it for him. Caressing his lover's face, he kissed him deeply, savoring the coolness the water had left behind. Stepping back, Ross admired the view. Scott's skin was covered in a sheen of sweat, his eyes shone, and his pupils were so dilated they appeared almost black. His cock was rock-hard and leaking from the tip.

"You've taken a lot tonight, so if you need to stop, give me the safeword," Ross said. "If you can take it, I'd like to flog you next."

"Yes, Sir. I'm back to green. I can take a flogging, Sir."

"You're such a good boy for me," Ross said as he reached out and gave Scott's erection a firm stroke. "I want you to try not to come from this next part. I'll tell you when you are allowed. Can you do that for me, sweetheart? If you get too close, let me know."

"Yes, Sir."

Picking up the flogger, Ross began to flog Scott's chest and abs. Scott began making the most delightful sounds as he squirmed on the cross. He was clearly more sensitive here. Grinning wickedly, Ross gently dragged the flogger over Scott's raging hard on, making him buck and cry out.

Next Ross flogged the front of each thigh, careful not to hit too close to his groin. The next time he lashed the flogger over Scott's chest, he cried out. "Yellow! I'm too close!"

"Good boy," Ross praised, taking a pause. Scott's cock was straining even more now, and his balls had started to draw up. "I love how wrecked you look, it's beautiful," Ross purred before stepping closer to ravish Scott's mouth.

After breaking the kiss, Ross stepped back and took a sip of water, waiting for Scott's testicles to relax. Then he started all over again, edging Scott to the brink and pulling him back from it. After the fifth time, Scott was weeping. "Please, Sir. Please let me come. *Please!*"

"Good boy," Ross commended. "Thank you for begging me so nicely. You may come this time."

Instead of picking up the flogger again, Ross fell to his knees before Scott and took his cock into his mouth. Scott yelped in surprise, and Ross smiled around the hard flesh. Tasting the salty bitterness of Scott's pre-come on his tongue, he held the tip of the cock in his mouth for a moment. He savored the weight of it as he massaged his tongue around the head.

As he ran his tongue along the frenulum, Scott shivered and groaned. Reaching up, Ross caressed Scott's scrotum, as he took more of the cock into his mouth. Relaxing his muscles, he pushed until the head breached the back of his throat, and he began to swallow around the intrusion. Ross was proud of his ability to deep throat. It's not a skill he used often, but it made for a delightful treat for his lovers.

Once again Scott began to get close to the edge, so Ross began to suck, sliding the cock in and out of his mouth, holding Scott's hips still with one hand and fondling his balls with the other. It didn't take long until Scott came, screaming his release and flooding Ross' mouth. He swallowed every drop until the cock stopped pulsing and the hardness slowly softened.

Getting up from his knees, Ross kissed Scott again, letting him taste himself on his tongue. It was a hard, filthy kiss that had Scott moaning.

"You're amazing," Ross said as he stepped back to appraise the wreck of a man he'd made. "Do you think you're ready to face Stuart tomorrow?"

"I hope so, Sir," Scott replied. "As long as I have you at my side."

"Don't worry, you will. Now how about I get you down from there and you get on your knees for me?" Ross suggested as he freed his own erection. "I want you to use that beautiful mouth on me."

Scott flicked his eyes from Ross' cock to his face and licked his lips. "I'd love to, Sir."

MISCALCULATION

Scott was fidgeting with his tie until Ross grabbed one of his hands. "Hey, remember what the doctor told you? Deep breaths and try not to get lost inside your head."

Nodding, Scott proceeded to breathe deeply while squeezing his hand. "Thanks, Sir. I'm trying to focus on the soreness of my ass, but it's not working as well today."

"Remember, Stuart can't hurt you. We're meeting him in my building, surrounded by my security guards. If you can control yourself and not flee from the building, no one else can grab you. You want to see him put in his place, don't you?"

"Yeah, I do," Scott agreed. "Although, I wish I didn't have to be there. Seeing him in person, after what he threatened to do to me..."

"We need to present a united front," Ross reminded him. "Also, this will help you face your fear head-on. You'll see, he's not so scary in person."

While Ross kept a firm hold of his hand, he couldn't help squirming in his seat. The welts from last night's session in the playroom ached pleasantly under his suit, and he kept wanting to press them into the seat to feel them more deeply.

"You need to stop squirming, or Stuart might get ideas," Ross teased.

"Don't you dare, I'm nervous enough as it is. The guy threatened to have my dick and balls cut off!" Scott reminded him.

"That dick and those balls are *mine*. He better not touch them, or he'll have a lot more to worry about than my exposure of his illicit business practices," Ross said with a growl.

Leaning over, Scott looked at Ross with adoration. "I love how possessive you are of me. I never thought I'd want that, but ... yeah, I love *belonging* to you. I love you, Sir."

"I love you too, you darling, skittish man," Ross said before pulling Scott in for a lingering kiss. "Now, what do you do if Stuart tries to scare you?"

"Take deep breaths and count to ten," Scott recalled. "And remind myself that your security guards will keep us both safe."

"That's exactly right. If we get through today unscathed, let's celebrate by vegging out and playing video games tomorrow? We can pig out on ice cream and pizza."

"That sounds wonderful."

* * *

As usual, Ross arrived fashionably late. Stuart was already there, flanked by two of his people. He had a scowl on his face as he watched them come in. Ross sat himself down at the far end of the table from Stuart, and Scott seated himself next to Ross.

"What is the meaning of this?" Stuart demanded. "I do not get *summoned* by the likes of you."

"Yet, here you are," Ross pointed out. "I take it my invitation must have piqued your interest?"

"Are you ready to sign over that land to me?" Stuart asked with a growl.

"You know very well that I'm not. You also know I've already broken ground on my project for Johnstown," Ross reminded him.

"Then we're done here," Stuart spat, rising from his chair.

"I wouldn't leave yet, if I were you," Ross said calmly. "Not if you don't want your entire operation dismantled and your ass thrown in jail."

Glaring at Ross, Stuart slowly sat back down. "What is this about? What could you possibly have to threaten me with?"

Ross produced a USB drive, sliding it across the table at Stuart. "That contains a copy of every illicit operation you are running that I was able to uncover. It includes your plans to improve your smuggling operation using the network of tunnels under the Johnstown neighborhood."

Stuart's face turned several shades of red and he was clearly struggling to come up with a rebuttal, but Ross didn't give him time to compose his thoughts.

"I have already informed the city planning office of the existence of those tunnels, which seem to be missing from the city records. I have filed for permits to use them myself, but as an efficient way to transport legal goods from the docks into the neighborhood. It will reduce traffic and pollution in the area. I plan to build a solar powered electric train system after my contractors reinforce all the tunnels."

"What do you want?" Stuart asked through gritted teeth.

"Simple. Back off. Leave Scott and myself alone and stop trying to get your hands on that land. Do that, and I won't expose you and report your dealings to the cops."

"How do I know you'll keep your word?"

"You know damn well I've always been a man of my word, and my reputation should tell you I will."

Stuart looked over at Scott. "I have no idea how you got away from my men. You spoiled everything, and I wish I could have had you neutered when I had the chance. A man like you running away from his soulmate doesn't deserve to keep his dick."

Scott's hand shot to his groin protectively while his heart rate sped up. He tried to remain calm by taking several deep breaths, while Ross reached out and put a hand on his shoulder, getting Scott to refocus on him. "He's baiting you, sweetheart."

Then he turned his attention to Stuart. "You apologize to my soulmate ... *sincerely* ... or I will ruin you," Ross growled.

With an exasperated sigh Stuart complied. "I apologize, Scott. That was ... unprofessional of me," Stuart said before glaring at Ross. "Happy now?"

A few more deep breaths and Scott nodded to Ross. "I'm fine."

"Okay," Ross said. "Stuart, I will give you the same timeframe you kept giving me. You have twenty-four hours to review what's on that USB and respond with a written and signed promise to not attempt any more threats against us in order to get your hands on that land. The city knows about the tunnel system, so it should be worthless to you now."

Snatching up the USB drive, Stuart begrudgingly agreed. "Alright. You will have your written promise. You've been a thorn in my side for too long and I'll gladly be done with this business. Will that be all?"

"I think that about covers it, yes. Thank you for your time, Mr. Grant."

Without saying another word, Stuart and his people got up and left. Scott let out a sigh of relief when they were gone. "That went better than I'd hoped."

"Yes," Ross said. "It makes me wonder what he's still hiding. He agreed far more quickly than I expected."

"Should we be worried?"

"*You* shouldn't be worried, but we should be wary. I'll make some phone calls first. Then how do you feel about going out to dinner?"

"That sounds great."

* * *

The next morning, they were finishing breakfast when a courier delivered a packet from Stuart Grant's office. "I'll need my lawyer to review this, but give me a moment to skim through it, okay?"

Scott nodded, taking a sip of his coffee.

Ross' face quickly went from neutral to horrified in a manner of seconds. "What's wrong, Sir?"

"*Shit!* That bastard," Ross said with a growl as he fished out his phone and dialed. "Yes, this is an emergency. My name is Ross Milgrave ... yes, *that* Ross Milgrave. The Johnstown neighborhood needs to be evacuated immediately. I own the land, and I've received a credible threat that there are explosives lining the tunnels under the entire area. I was just informed that they are going to be detonated. *Today.*"

Scott's heart leaped into his throat when his mind processed what Ross said. *Shit.*

Ross spent a while on the phone with the emergency operator. When he was done, he made several more calls. Scott sat in stunned silence. They knew Stuart's compliance was too good to be true, but to go this far? There were thousands of people who lived and worked in Johnstown. They would be left unemployed, homeless, or worse, if Stuart managed to detonate explosives in those tunnels. *Can all those people get evacuated in time?* Scott wondered.

While Ross was still on the phone, Scott picked up the paperwork he had been looking at. On top was a letter from Stuart.

Ross,

Attached you will find the required documents you requested. I have agreed to not harm you or that ungrateful soulmate of yours, and I relinquish all claims I had on the Johnstown neighborhood.

However, you did not ask me to leave Johnstown unscathed. Since I cannot have it, neither can you. As a contingency plan, I had all those old tunnels laced with explosives months ago. I will have them detonated precisely at noon today. I suggest you try to evacuate the poor souls living there.

Go ahead and expose me for this. Without the acquisition of Johnstown, you've effectively ruined me. By the time you receive this, it won't matter anymore. I'm leaving the country and you'll never find me.

Have a pleasant day,

That would give emergency workers only a few hours to evacuate the area. It was going to be chaos.

Ross was still on the phone, talking to someone excitedly, when he looked up at Scott. "We need to turn on the TV!"

They both rushed out of the dining room. Ross turned on the TV and switched to the all-news channel. Currently, they were giving the local weather forecast, but about a minute later the weatherman was interrupted.

"Ladies and gentlemen, we've just received some very serious news regarding the Johnstown neighborhood. There is a network of recently discovered tunnels all below the region, and it's being reported that the tunnels are lined with explosives. Everyone who is currently in the area of Johnstown is asked to quickly and calmly evacuate the area until further notice. I repeat, anyone who is in the area of Johnstown is being asked to evacuate, immediately."

"Good. They should be broadcasting this over all the local radio stations as well," Ross said.

"Is there anything I can do?" Scott asked.

Thinking for a moment, Ross nodded. "Yeah, while I call the police and fill them in on what's going on and who is responsible, you can call the contractors that have been working on the tunnels. Ask them if they have seen anything suspicious down there. Maybe we can isolate or minimize the problem."

"Sure, how do I contact them?"

"Go to the study and login to my laptop, you'll find a file with all the contractors names and contact information in the Milgrave-Hansen Project folder."

"Got it."

Making his way to the study, Scott's mind raced. He hoped that they could beat the clock and mitigate this disaster. Spending the next hour on the phone, Scott called every contractor on the list.

After he finished all the calls, he made his way back to the living room to find Ross, who was still watching the news and simultaneously texting someone on his phone.

"What's the situation? How's the evacuation going?"

"Too slow. People don't want to leave. Some folks think it's a hoax, others don't care. They've only managed to evacuate about a quarter of the people so far."

Scott was about to share what he'd learned from the contractors when the TV caught both of their attention.

"Breaking news! The man believed to be responsible for the explosives threatening the Johnstown neighborhood has been apprehended. He was attempting to flee the country, but his plane was delayed due to a mechanical failure. More on this story when further information has been released."

"Wow," Scott exclaimed.

"Yeah. I was not expecting that," Ross agreed before muting the TV. "So, what did you learn from the contractors?"

"Not all of them had crews down in the tunnels. Those that did hadn't noticed anything glaringly obvious, but one guy did say his crew had mentioned seeing a series of black, plastic containers affixed at regular intervals along the tunnel walls. They had no idea what they could be and opted not to touch them."

"Those could be the explosives, let me call the police back and let them know."

Another half-hour passed as they watched the news reports. More people were convinced to evacuate, and a small army of fire, ambulance, and other rescue vehicles were positioned outside of the estimated blast zone.

Ross' phone rang. "Hello? Yes, I reported that about thirty minutes ago. They are? Can they get them all? Alright, thanks for the update."

Scott looked at Ross expectantly.

"That was the chief of police. They found the black boxes. Each one contains a single bomb, set to detonate by remote. They are trying to dismantle and disarm as many as they can. They have several bomb squads working down in the tunnels, prioritizing the areas where the most residents who haven't evacuated still are."

"Can they get them all in time?"

Shaking his head, Ross said. "Sadly, no. They've been working on them since they found them. It would take days to get them all. The tunnel network is extensive."

"That bastard. What did he hope to gain from doing this?"

"Nothing. This was his way of saying *fuck you* to us."

"Hey, that's your photo," Scott gestured at the TV screen. Ross unmuted.

"*—billionaire real estate developer Ross Milgrave reportedly alerted the authorities of this threat to the Johnstown neighborhood. Based on verified records, he owns the land that the neighborhood is built on and is currently underway with a redevelopment project for this community. Speculations are running rampant as to how he and Stuart Grant are connected and whether Ross Milgrave may also be in on this bomb threat. More—*"

Scott was in shock. "Do they actually believe you might be working *with* Stuart?"

Before Ross could reply, his phone rang again. He spoke for several tense moments on the phone before getting up. "We're going down there."

"What? Why?"

"That was the head of my PR department. Rumors about me are spreading like wildfire because I haven't been there to field questions from reporters. I wanted to coordinate this from behind the scenes and not make this about me. I guess I don't have a choice now."

MITIGATING A TRAGEDY

Ross was texting strategy ideas between himself and the head of his PR department. They'd arrive at the safe perimeter outside of Johnstown in about ten minutes, and he was preparing to speak with reporters.

He had always known that Stuart was a sociopath, but he never thought the man would go this far. Ross' only consolation was that Stuart had been caught before he'd had a chance to flee. Once this immediate crisis was over, Ross would give all the evidence he had against the man to the authorities. That should put Stuart in prison for a very long time.

Looking over at Scott, he reached out to still his bouncing knee. "Hey, we'll be fine. The reporters are set up outside of the estimated blast radius."

"Yeah, I know," Scott said. "I'm sorry that I'm anxious, but what if Stuart manages to drag you down with him?"

"I won't let that happen. I have enough evidence against him, and nothing leads back to me other than his threats. Not that it should, but I made sure of it."

"Okay. I'd hate to see you get accused for being in collusion with him, after everything he's done to us."

"I'll send all the evidence against him to the chief of police and the district attorney, including your kidnapping. If it had only been the blackmail, I might understand people still being suspicious. But when he kidnapped and threatened you with bodily harm, he crossed a line. The public will demonize him for that."

"Okay. I'll try not to worry about it too much right now, Sir."

The limousine slowed and stopped. Ross only now realized he had never changed and was still casually dressed in jeans and a sweater, as was Scott. Normally, he made sure he was in a suit and tie. *Oh well, nothing we can do about it now.*

Stepping out of the limousine, Ross took Scott's hand and made his way toward the reporters, some of whom were live on the air, giving updates to their various affiliates. When they noticed Ross and Scott, many scrambled and redirected their attention to them. Ross felt Scott tense up next to him and he gently squeezed his hand.

The reporters asked a flurry of questions and Ross raised his hand to ask for silence. "I'm here to aid in whatever way I can in the evacuation efforts and to set the record straight. There isn't much time, so I will be brief. Yes, I own the land that the Johnstown neighborhood is built on. I bought it some years ago with the hopes of redeveloping the area and improving the lives of everyone who lives here.

"This is not widely known, but I grew up in Johnstown. This community may be rough around the edges, but the people who live here are tough, honest, hardworking people. I won't get into the details now about why this is happening, but it is in part my fault," Ross confessed. "For that I'm sorry. Stuart Grant has been trying to find ways to take this land from me, and I didn't want him to get his hands on my old neighborhood. I know what he does when he redevelops an area. Unfortunately, my efforts to keep Stuart from taking ownership of this land has, in part, led to the situation here today. The people in Johnstown don't deserve what is happening. They are innocent victims of this feud between us.

"Whatever happens here today, I pledge to you now, that I will work with the residents to rebuild Johnstown. The residents' needs will remain my priority, as they have always been. Any profits from the redevelopment will be used to help *all* residents and businesses rebuild. Also, I promise all medical, or perish the thought, funeral expenses, will be paid for.

"Once the crisis is over, I'll gladly hold a press conference and give more detailed information. Right now, let's all help get as many people to safety as possible. Buildings can be rebuilt, but lives cannot. That's the priority right now."

There was silence for several beats as the reporters processed everything that was said. Then they turned back toward their cameras, urging the residents of Johnstown who hadn't evacuated yet to get out quickly. There was barely an hour left before the bombs were set to go off.

Moving away from the reporters and still clutching Scott's hand firmly, Ross made his way over to where the emergency responders were set up. "Is there anything we can do to help?"

The cop Ross addressed looked at him sternly. "No civilians are allowed, please step back, sir."

Ignoring the order, he pressed on. "I'm Ross Milgrave, the owner of the land that Johnstown is built on. How much progress have they made in disarming the bombs?"

The man's demeanor immediately changed. "I'm sorry, I didn't recognize you, Mr. Milgrave. The progress has been slow, but thankfully each bomb is wired the same way. So, once we figured out how to disarm the trigger mechanism on one, disarming the rest was easier. The problem is, there are too many of them."

"I heard. Sadly, Stuart has been planning this for a long time. No wonder he's been so aggressive in trying to get me to sign over the land to him," Ross said with a sigh. "Please, is there anything that Scott or I can do to assist?"

"Do you have any way to help the evacuees? They're going to need shelter, food, and clothes. The Red Cross is looking for a place to set all that up," the man explained.

"I know the perfect place," Ross said. "I have that new high-rise downtown. It passed inspection last week and we haven't officially opened it yet because we were still negotiating all the leases. There is a lot of room in there. Half of the building has dedicated office space that can be used for triage if necessary, but the other half has apartments, complete with kitchens and bathrooms. They aren't furnished, but it's a start."

"Perfect," the man said as he flagged over someone. "This is Katrina. She is our local Red Cross coordinator. Work with her on setting up the shelter for the residents."

Ross told Katrina what he'd told the other man, and the woman was thrilled. "That's so generous of you to offer that space. Can I send a team ahead to assess everything?"

"Yes, absolutely! Scott? Can you go with them, please?" Ross asked. "I'll send you all my access codes into the building, and I'll call the head of security and let him know to expect you."

Scott nodded. "You can count on me, Sir."

Smiling at Ross he pulled him in for a quick, chaste kiss. "I know I can, sweetheart. Stay in touch, please."

"Yes, Sir," Scott replied.

Once Scott was off with the Red Cross team, Ross immediately dialed the head of security at Milgrave Tower. "Hey, Brad? This is Ross. I wanted to alert you that my soulmate, Scott Hansen, is on his way over with a Red Cross team. I'm going to repurpose the building temporarily as a shelter for the Johnstown residents. I'm sending him all the access codes. Please help Scott coordinate the Red Cross team, along with the residents when they arrive."

"Yes sir. Thanks for the head's up!"

Hanging up the phone, Ross pulled up the access codes he'd stored and sent them to Scott in a text message. Once that was completed, he refocused on working with Katrina.

"What else do you need?" Ross asked.

"Once I hear back from my team, we should start transporting everyone we've evacuated so far. I could use your help in getting some buses," Katrina suggested.

"I'll get right on it."

Ross called his team back at the office. They could help hire the buses needed. Once that was accomplished, Ross helped Katrina hand out supplies to the evacuees who had been streaming into the staging area for some hours now. Once the buses began to arrive, he stepped up to help the evacuees board them in an orderly fashion, while making sure the drivers knew exactly where they were going.

"Where are you sending us?" one resident asked.

"I have an empty building filled with apartments downtown. We're sending you all there for the time being. Don't worry, I'll make sure you have everything you need until this is over," Ross reassured her.

"Why are you being so generous?" another resident asked.

"I can't turn my backs on all of you now. I grew up here, and while I may not live in Johnstown anymore, it's part of my roots. I need to make sure you're all okay," Ross explained.

One after the other, he continued to help get the residents onto the buses as they arrived, while trying to reassure them that it would be okay. Checking in with his team, he was pleased that they managed to hire about one hundred and fifty buses. That should be able to accommodate the entire population of Johnstown of approximately ten thousand residents.

When it reached 11:45am, the bomb squads also evacuated and joined them in the safe zone. Ross ran over to the head of the bomb squad team when he saw them. "Are there any more people left in the neighborhood? We still have several more buses we could fill."

"It looks like most people have made it out and we managed to talk some stragglers into coming with us," the man replied. "However, we need to move the staging area back farther ... I think we're still too close to the potential blast radius. We discovered that many of the bombs are directly below natural gas lines and the explosion could be larger than we originally feared."

Immediately the call went out and everyone began to move back, leaving behind vehicles, equipment, and tents. The remaining buses were told to move back while everyone else just began to run. Thankfully they had managed to get all the elderly and infirm evacuees onto the buses already, so most of the residents who were left were able to go on foot for now.

They were still retreating when the bombs went off, causing the ground to shake and knocking many people off their feet. Ross barely managed to keep his own balance as he helped those around him back onto their feet. The cloud of dust that rose in the air behind them blocked out the sun almost instantly and their world turned gray as the dust and ash began to rain down moments later.

Ross felt his phone buzz, and he pulled it out of his pocket while continuing to retreat, supporting one evacuee along the way. "Hey Scott, how are things going?"

"They're fine. We're getting people settled in. Are you okay? We could see the explosion from here."

"I'm a little shaken up, but I'm fine. We're all retreating to get away from the blast zone and the ash and dust that's raining down. I'll join you there once I help get the last of the evacuees on their way to you."

"Okay, sounds good. I'm so glad you're okay, Sir. I love you."

"I love you, too." Ross smiled as he put his phone back into his pocket and kept moving. Scott had come a long way from the skittish man who ran away from him the first night they met. It warmed his heart to know that Scott worried for him.

* * *

Several hours later and all the evacuees were now being settled into the apartments in Milgrave Tower. The Red Cross was set up in the lobby, helping to get each person or family into one of the apartments. There were around one thousand apartments in the building, ranging in size from small studios to large three-bedrooms. Ross had gotten his building manager to bring over a complete set of plans for the building, so they could assign apartments based on need, trying not to split up families.

Ross arrived at the high-rise and was looking around for Scott when he saw Katrina. "Have you seen Scott?"

"He was escorting a couple to their assigned apartment," she explained. "He should be back down soon."

"Good, how are things going? Have you gotten any casualty reports yet?"

Shaking her head, she said. "No. I've been busy coordinating the efforts here, so I haven't checked in with the emergency responders for a while."

"When Scott gets back, ask him to meet me in the conference room, please."

Making his way down the hall, Ross stopped at a station where someone had set out portable coffee dispensers and poured himself a cup. Once in the conference room, he turned on the TV that was hanging on the far wall and tuned in to see the latest news report.

Aerial footage showed the devastation of the area on screen. Many of the buildings were turned to rubble, some of the land had collapsed down into the underlying tunnels, and whole areas had flooded. It looked like only a quarter of the buildings still stood, in the area where they had managed to disarm the bombs. Still, the entire neighborhood looked completely uninhabitable. *Damn it, Stuart, why the fuck would you do this to these people?*

"—Johnstown was devastated by an explosion earlier today. Bombs were found in a previously unknown tunnel system under the neighborhood. Thankfully, most residents managed to evacuate the area, but it is estimated that there may be dozens, if not hundreds, of casualties."

"Shit," Ross said aloud.

"Hey," came a tired voice, before a hand closed over his shoulder. "You saved thousands of people by calling it in when you did."

Looking up to see Scott, Ross made a half-hearted effort to smile. "Yeah, I know, but we should have been able to save them all. Damn Stuart and his obsession over this stupid piece of dirt."

"You couldn't have known he'd go this far," Scott reassured him.

"That isn't much consolation."

"What are you going to do?"

"The only thing I *can* do. Fix this. It's going to cost a lot more money, but I'll rebuild Johnstown. I'll make it even better than we had planned to and in the meantime all the residents can keep staying here. I will push back the opening of this building until I've restored all these people's homes and businesses."

"Wow, can you afford to do all that?" Scott asked as he sat down in a chair next to Ross.

"I can't afford not to. I made a promise to the people of Johnstown that I'd improve their neighborhood. I can't back out on that promise now. I've built up this massive fortune, I may as well put it to good use."

Katrina came in to join them. "We have moved in the last of the evacuees. You should both go home, there isn't much else you can do for these people tonight."

Suddenly realizing how weary he was, Ross nodded. "You're right. Let's get some rest and I can start drawing up plans tomorrow."

"What plans?" Katrina asked out of curiosity.

"I need to re-evaluate the Milgrave-Hansen Project. It's obviously going to take a lot more work now, but I need to start planning how to restore the Johnstown neighborhood," Ross replied. "I will also need to get my teams in there as soon as possible to assess the situation."

"You plan to continue with your redevelopment project, despite what happened?" Katrina asked.

"Yes, of course. I still own the land, and I have a contract with the neighborhood development council. It's going to cost a lot more, but I see no reason to back out of that agreement."

"It's good to meet someone of your social standing that isn't out to stab the little guy. You're being remarkably generous to all these people," Katrina said.

"I used to be one of them. I grew up in Johnstown. I'm not going to abandon them now," Ross said.

"Well, you may have restored my faith in humanity, Mr. Milgrave," Katrina said as she turned to leave. "Thank you again for everything you've done so far."

"Come on Scott, let's go home," Ross said as he stood and took Scott's hand in his. "It's past time for your daily spanking, and I could use a soak in the hot tub and some sleep."

"That sounds perfect, Sir."

THE SOUL IMPACT

Scott found himself helping the evacuees at the high-rise while Ross busied himself with plans for restoring the Johnstown neighborhood. They were being heralded as heroes, having alerted authorities with enough time to get most of the residents out. The final casualty count was seventy-six dead and a few dozen injured. Any single loss was tragic, but it could have been much worse.

It took three months for the extent of the damage to be assessed and for Ross and his team to come up with an entirely new plan for Johnstown. They had to take into account all the areas with collapsed tunnels that would need to be rebuilt or repurposed. In the meantime, Stuart Grant accepted a plea deal from the district attorney, taking all responsibility of his actions upon himself. He was given several consecutive life sentences while his daughter stepped forward to take control of his company and all assets.

The first thing that Lenora Grant did was offer a public apology for her father's actions, and to outline a plan that completely restructured Grant Holdings, Inc. Afterward, she invited Ross and Scott to dinner and privately apologized to both as well.

Ross had presented his plans to the residents of Johnstown in one of the large unoccupied office floors in the high-rise. The presentation was broadcast to every resident's television and recorded for later viewing. The residents were given a month to deliberate amongst themselves over the proposal before giving their feedback.

In the meantime, word of all that Ross and Scott had done during the crisis had spread. Residents had been filming them and posting videos online. Several videos went viral, mostly of Ross or Scott carrying crying children, helping to reunite them with their families.

Any lingering negative sentiment toward Scott for fleeing Ross on their first meeting disappeared after that. They were heralded as the *Saviors of Johnstown*, and Ross took advantage by resuming their interrupted press tour. Now that the plans for Johnstown was in the hands of residents, they had the time to get away. Scott wished they could skip it entirely, but it was best to just get it over with.

* * *

They were on their last stop of the press tour before heading back home. Scott was exhausted, but happy. Not one interviewer had brought up his panic disorder or how he had initially run from Ross. Instead they seemed more interested in the Johnstown neighborhood restoration.

In the dressing room before their final interview, Scott was pacing anxiously when Ross grabbed his hand. "Drop your pants and get over my knees, sweetheart."

"We're about to go on," Scott protested.

"Scott, you know we have at least five minutes before we're called. *Get over my knees.*"

Taking a breath and swallowing, Scott complied. "Yes, Sir."

As soon as he was perched over Ross' knees, he was being spanked in earnest. As each swat fell, Scott felt his anxiety retreat and his body relaxed over Ross' lap. After a couple of minutes of having his ass warmed, he was feeling much better.

"Okay, up you get," Ross said, as he stopped and gave Scott's ass one quick squeeze. "Put yourself together and don't squirm when we're on the air. Remember, this is a television interview."

"How am I supposed to not squirm when you spanked my ass red?" Scott asked as he rubbed his stinging behind.

"Don't tempt me, or I'll take you over my knee on live television," Ross teased.

"You wouldn't dare!"

"Scott, you've seen other guests on these shows do it, so don't think I won't," Ross said with all sincerity.

"You mean those were real spankings? I always thought they were playing around."

A knock came on their door. "One minute!" said the knocker.

Ross stood and smoothed over Scott's suit jacket and straightened his tie. "*Behave.*"

"Yes, Sir."

Leaving the dressing room with his hand in Ross', they were led toward the stage and told to wait until they had been introduced. When they made their way on stage, they smiled and waved to the studio audience, while Scott tried not to squint at the bright stage lights. After having done dozens of radio and television interviews across the country, Scott was glad this would be the final one. *I can't wait to be back home.*

The host, Nelson Stone, had them seated next to each other on a very uncomfortable sofa. Scott tried not to wince as he sat his still stinging ass down.

"Welcome to *The Soul Impact*, gentlemen! I'm so happy to have you on our show today. You both have quite the story to tell," Nelson began.

"We're happy to be here," Ross replied.

When Scott remained silent for a beat too long, Ross nudged him. "Oh, Yes. Thank you for having us!"

"You've both been sharing your incredible journeys and how you handled dealing with that awful crisis back in your hometown. Ross, you grew up in that neighborhood, isn't that right?"

Ross nodded. "Yes. I was born and raised there."

"In keeping with the theme of our show, I'd like to focus on something a little different. I'm sure you're both tired of answering the same questions over and over, am I right?"

"We're happy to share any part of our stories again, aren't we Scott?" Ross said as he reached around and put an arm around Scott's shoulders.

"Yes, of course. Anything you want to know," Scott agreed.

"Well, I hear that you both decided to enter into a formal domestic discipline relationship. Is that true?"

Scott could feel the heat rise on his face at the implication of where this interview was headed. *Oh no, please not this.*

"Yes, that's right Nelson," Ross replied. "I have always preferred being the dominant in relationships, and Scott is a natural submissive. This arrangement has helped Scott control aspects of his panic disorder, hasn't it, sweetheart?"

Why are we talking about this on live television? "Um, yeah. It has helped."

"Is that how you address your partner?" Nelson asked. "I'm a bit surprised at how casual he is."

Ross turned his gaze on Scott, causing the heat to rise in his face. "Oh, I'm sorry ... I wasn't expecting to talk about this in public. I'm sorry, Sir."

"That's better," Ross said. "You have to forgive Scott. He was a bit anxious about this interview and I had to turn him over my knees in the dressing room a few moments ago."

Some cheers and whoops came from the audience at that admission and Scott's heart began to race. When his breathing picked up, Ross noticed. "Sweetheart, are you having a panic attack?"

Fuck, no. Not here. Please don't do this here. Scott shook his head. "No, Sir. I ... I'm fine, Sir."

"Sweetheart, you shouldn't lie to me. I can see you're going into a panic," Ross admonished as he tightened his arm around Scott's shoulders.

"Do you need to discipline him? We have a special set up just for that," Nelson said gleefully.

Scott turned around as a curtain was raised to reveal a spanking horse and a stand lined with implements. *What? No!*

Ross tightened his grip around his shoulders. "That's a lovely set up. I take it your guests discipline their soulmates on this show often?"

"That's why my show is called *The Soul Impact!*"

Groaning, Scott hung his head. *This is happening, isn't it?*

"I will give you a choice, Scott," Ross said, turning to him. "Bend over that horse and take ten from the paddle, or when we get home, you take twenty-five from a switch."

"I've never been switched before, Sir," Scott said.

"I know you haven't. Still, I ask you to make a choice, or I will ask the host to decide on a fitting form of discipline."

Shit. The thought of being punished here was terrifying, but the switch was still on his *maybe* list of limits. If he didn't decide, whatever the host decided might be even worse.

"May I ask a question first, Sir?"

Ross nodded. "One question, go ahead."

"Which way will you ask me to bend over the horse? Facing the audience or away?"

"Nelson, what do you think? Would your audience like to watch me redden his pretty ass? Or would they rather see his reactions to getting a sound paddling?"

The audience erupted in whoops and hollers as they shouted. Some cried out "ass!" while others cried "face!"

Nelson waited for the audience to quiet before responding. "The audience seems evenly split. Personally? I love watching an ass being warmed, so that's my vote."

Sighing, Scott looked at Ross. "Okay. I'll choose ten with a paddle here, Sir."

"Good choice, sweetheart," Ross praised. "Nelson, do you permit bare buttocks, or should he keep his pants on?"

"We air this late because I think bare would be preferred by all."

No, not all, Scott grumbled to himself.

"Sweetheart, please go to the spanking horse, pull down your pants and bend over it, ass facing the audience."

"Yes, Sir."

Making his way over to the horse amid the cheers of the audience, he waited until he was right in front of the horse with his back turned before he exposed his already pink ass and bent over.

Ross was right behind him, giving him a quick, friendly swat as he went to pick up one of several paddles hanging from a set of implements.

Nelson joined them. "We need to cut for a quick commercial break. Stay tuned to watch Ross Milgrave give his soulmate Scott Hansen a little domestic discipline!"

Wait, what?

Chuckling behind him, Ross smoothed his hand over his ass. "May I warm him up with my hand while we're on the commercial break?"

"What? No! You already spanked my ass backstage!" Scott protested.

"Scott, don't make me add to your count," Ross warned.

"Sure!" Nelson said with enthusiasm. "Watch the red light over the camera. When it starts to blink, you get ten seconds before we're on the air again."

Without further ado, Scott felt Ross' hand land a smack onto his already spanked ass. The skin was still tender, so he felt it more than he normally would. Thankfully, Ross wasn't spanking as forcefully as he had earlier. Scott realized that what Ross was doing was mostly putting on a show for the live audience while they waited for the end of the commercial break.

It seemed to go on for an eternity before Ross stopped and gave him a warning. "Get ready, sweetheart."

"Welcome back to *The Soul Impact!*" Nelson began. He reminded the audience who the guests were and what was about to happen. "Take it away Ross. Give him a good paddling for trying to lie to you earlier."

"With pleasure," Ross said before the first blow landed. "Don't forget to count them, sweetheart."

The stinging of the impact had Scott trying to speak through gritted teeth. "One. I'm sorry, Sir." The blows kept landing as Scott counted and apologized. He barely contained a scream at the last hit. "Ten! I ... I'm so sorry, Sir."

"Good boy, you took that well. I'm so proud of you sweetheart," Ross said as he helped pull Scott's pants back up and to stand upright. After wiping away his tears and giving him a quick kiss, he guided Scott back to the sofa where Nelson was waiting.

"You really know how to handle a paddle, Ross. That was impressive. I hope you appreciate how easy you got off tonight, Scott," Nelson said.

"I will probably appreciate it more the first time he decides to take a switch to my ass," Scott said as he sat gingerly next to Ross, unable to hide his wince this time.

"Oh, I guarantee that will happen someday," Ross promised as the audience laughed.

"That's about all the time we have tonight. Thank you again for joining us Ross and Scott. It's been an absolute pleasure!"

* * *

Back in Ross' private jet, he had Scott strip bare, so he could apply some soothing balm to Scott's well-disciplined rear.

"Thank you for doing that. I know we kind of sprung that whole public discipline on you at the last minute, but they insisted you didn't know. They prefer getting genuine reactions from guests."

"You didn't ask me my color this time," Scott pouted. "You always do."

"I know. They also asked I didn't mention safewords, but if you had used yours at any point, I would have stopped," Ross explained as he rubbed the balm over his heated skin. "That's also why I gave you the choice. I knew you could handle ten from a paddle. I've seen you take worse without using your safeword."

"Yeah, you're right, Sir. It wasn't that bad. The worst of it was having to do it in front of all those people. That was the punishment, more than the paddling."

"Yes, that was the point, and you got through it beautifully, without me even having to restrain you," Ross praised. "I'm proud of you, sweetheart."

"I did start to panic," Scott admitted. "But then having to decide between punishments or letting the host decide? It snapped me out of it instead of making it worse."

"I'm glad to hear that. I was hoping that spankings would have a positive effect on you and help with your panic attacks. I talked at length with Dr. Landry about it, and I made some tweaks to our contract before I presented it to you the first time."

"So that's why he's been holding off prescribing any additional medication to me?"

"He wanted to see how well the discipline might help first. If it's not enough, there are still always other medication options."

"Okay, good to know, Sir."

"We still have several hours before we land, sweetheart," Ross purred into his ear. His hands went back to massaging his ass, adding some more balm. "What could we possibly do to kill some time?"

Rolling his eyes, Scott turned around. "I don't know ... get some sleep?" Scott teased.

"We can sleep when we're back home," Ross said as he pushed a button that changed the configuration of the seats into a small bed. Scott yelped as he was pushed down roughly and straddled. "I have other plans for you."

Scott laughed and pulled Ross down for a kiss before letting his soulmate ravish him repeatedly at 40,000 feet.

LOOSE ENDS

Ross and Scott were meeting with the residents of Johnstown today. They were ready to provide feedback on the proposal for restoring the neighborhood. He knew the residents would want to make at least some changes to the proposed plan. A lot of careful planning had gone into the proposal, but Ross was always interested to see how the plans could be improved.

The residents filed into the space, and Ross knew they had named a representative to speak for them. Several large monitors were set up to display a digital representation of the rebuilt Johnstown, so it would be easier for everyone to visualize what was being discussed.

Once everyone was gathered, Ross stepped forward. "Welcome. I hope you had enough time to review the plans. I am eager to hear your feedback and I'm open to considering any changes you may wish to ask for. You are the ones who will be living here once the restoration has been completed."

An older woman stepped up to the microphone. "I'm Mildred Donovan. I've been asked to be the spokesperson for the residents of Johnstown. First, we wanted to thank you, Mr. Milgrave. You saved so many of us with your quick actions, you've given us shelter in our time of need, and you're helping to rebuild our neighborhood. We truly cannot thank you enough for your generosity."

"Thank you, Mildred. As you all know, I grew up in Johnstown. I feel I have an obligation to take care of my own. None of you asked for what happened. You got caught up in this ridiculous feud between Stuart Grant and myself. You deserve better."

"I remember you and your parents," Mildred said. "I ran the little dry cleaner around the corner from your place. What happened to them was such a tragedy. When you purchased the land that Johnstown was built on, I knew you would do right by us."

Ross felt his face flush. "Thanks Mildred. Now, I know we're not all here to pile praise on me. I want to hear what your concerns are, regarding the plans for your neighborhood."

"I have everything written down here," Mildred said as she adjusted her glasses. She methodically went through each point of concern and Ross made sure to highlight each on the large digital map of the area. After each concern was voiced, Ross took notes. In some cases, he explained why they couldn't change certain plans, either due to building codes or irreparable structural damage that was caused by the explosions and subsequent flooding.

Many of the requests they had were perfectly reasonable, such as widening the sidewalks, so pedestrians weren't so close to traffic. Ross took extensive notes and promised to incorporate as many of the suggested changes that he could.

"Thank you everyone. I will have my team work on modifying the proposal and send it back to the residents with the changes. Once we have finalized the plans, we can then give you a timeline for when it's completed, and you can all go back home."

Cheers rose from the group. It couldn't have been easy for them to adjust to being crammed together in a high-rise like they currently were, but he knew they were making the best of it.

* * *

After everyone had cleared out, Ross turned to Scott and took his hand. "Come on, let me take you out to dinner."

Leading Scott out of the building, Ross decided to walk. The restaurant he had in mind was only a few blocks away, and the evening was clear and mild. Scott paused when they neared their destination. "Are you taking me to where we had our first *date*?"

"Yeah. I thought it would be nice to go back and ... I dunno ... reminisce a little. We've been through so much since then."

They went in and Ross was happy to see that the same booth they had sat in last time was unoccupied. Once they were seated, a waitress came over to hand them some menus. "Can I get you two something ... oh my, aren't you ... aren't you...?"

Chuckling at being recognized, Ross nodded. "Yes, we are. Scott and I had our first date here. I was feeling nostalgic tonight, and as I recall, you make the best burgers in town."

"Oh, yes sir! Are you both ready to order?"

They placed their order and the flustered waitress flitted off. Ross then took Scott's hands in his. "We've both been so busy lately. I appreciate all the work you've been putting in to help the Johnstown residents. I've wanted to ask if you plan to get back to writing anytime soon?"

"I'd like to, Sir. I have a million ideas for new stories after everything that's happened. I haven't yet because it felt … selfish? These people need all the help they can get while they are displaced, and with having you as my soulmate … well it's not like I need the income."

"Sweetheart, I love you. If you want to go back to writing, I can bring someone else in to take over and help until Johnstown has been rebuilt. Writing is your passion and you should get back to it if you're ready."

Squeezing his hands, Scott smiled. "Are you sure? Helping these people feels like the right thing to do. I keep putting my publisher off whenever they ask when I'm going to start a new novel. Apparently the last one has been flying off the shelves, especially after we completed our press tour."

"How about a compromise? Help out with the Johnstown residents a couple days each week and then spend the rest of the week writing."

Scott's face lit up at the suggestion. "That's perfect! Why hadn't I thought of that?"

"Probably because you think too much in absolutes?" Ross teased.

"Oh, yeah. I guess I do, Sir," Scott admitted, a lovely pink creeping over his cheeks.

"See, that's why you need me."

✳ ✳ ✳

A few weeks later, they were both able to sleep in, neither of them having any urgent plans that day. Sipping his cup of coffee, Ross admired Scott from across the table. *I think it's time.*

"Hey, want to go for a walk in the woods? It looks like a gorgeous day out there."

"Yeah, that sounds great, Sir. Let me go get changed."

Ross was already dressed for a hike, so he went to his study and fished out a new set of keys from his desk drawer, along with a small folio that he tucked into the inner pocket of the jacket he wore. Scott popped in a moment later, obviously eager to stretch his legs.

Ross took Scott's hand, and they made their way out of the house. At first, Ross made it look like he was meandering, although he had a specific destination in mind. However, before getting there, he had something to tell Scott.

They rounded a bend right where an old tree had fallen. Ross slowed and led Scott over to the tree and sat down. Scott looked at him confused before sitting next to him. "Why are we stopping, Sir?"

Taking a deep breath, Ross pulled the folio out of his jacket. "Do you remember the guy I hired to find dirt on Stuart? Well … I also asked him to do some digging on your dad, too."

Scott's breath hitched as his eyes flicked from his face down to the folio and back again. "What … what did he find out?"

"I'm so sorry, Scott. Your father passed away. In fact, according to the records, his body was found a few days after your mother had passed."

Sitting in stunned silence for a moment, Scott stared down at the folio, too afraid to reach out for it. "Do they know how he died?"

"His official cause of death was from stress cardiomyopathy. His mark had faded and based on the high levels of stress hormones in his system, they theorized that he'd died of a broken heart."

Tears slid down Scott's face as he looked back up at Ross. "He ... he still loved her? Then why...?"

Pulling Scott into is arms Ross embraced his soulmate. "I'm so sorry Scott. I know you wanted more closure than this. They only found a postcard in his pocket."

"A postcard? Do you have it?"

Ross let go of Scott and pulled the postcard out of the folio, handing it to him. "I didn't read it. I ... felt it was private."

"Thanks," Scott said as he took the card and stared at the picture on the front. "He ... was in Vancouver?"

"Yeah," Ross confirmed.

Turning the postcard over, Scott began to read the short message scrawled there.

"It's ... addressed to my mom. Dated on the day she died," Scott sobbed out, handing the postcard to Ross with a shaky hand.

Ross took the postcard. "May I?"

Scott nodded and buried his head into Ross' shoulder.

Dearest,

My soulmark began to fade today and that can only mean one thing. My love, I'm so sorry. I was a coward for running from you and our child and a bigger coward for never coming back. I was never good enough for you. You deserved so much better than me. I know you'll never get to read this, but I needed to write this down.

I love you.

Ross felt a well of emotion as tears pricked at the corner of his eyes. Letting the postcard flutter to the ground he held Scott tightly as he clung to him, wracked with sobs.

After Scott had calmed down, Ross pleaded. "Please Scott. Please never run from me like that. Promise me. I don't think I could bear it."

Taking several deep breaths Scott sat back up and looked at Ross. "I promise, Ross. I … I couldn't do that to you. I wouldn't. I'm sorry I tried before, but you've shown me that I'm worthy of your love. I love you. More than words could ever express."

"I love you, too," Ross replied as he cupped Scott's face and wiped his tears gently before drawing him into a kiss. "Now, why don't we finish our walk, hmm?"

Bending down to pick up the postcard, Ross tucked it back into the folio. "I'll give this to you when we get back. You can do whatever you want with it."

They started walking again, and Scott slipped his hand into Ross'. "Yeah, thanks. That hit me a lot harder than I thought it would, but … thank you. At least I know what happened to him now."

Changing the subject Ross started asking Scott about his latest novel. They discussed it at length, and Scott was telling him the plot twist he'd recently thought to add when he stopped with a gasp, causing Ross to grin. "Like it?"

They had rounded another bend that opened to where Ross had been building the writing retreat for Scott. It was a cozy little cabin; with all the amenities he would need. "Wow, this looks amazing! When did you have this built?"

"I started drawing the plans up the day after we talked about it. It was finished a couple of weeks ago. I've wanted to take you out here, but with everything going on, this was the first opportunity," Ross explained as he fished into his jeans pocket for the keys. "Come on, let me show you."

Leading Scott up the steps onto the small covered porch, he went to unlock the front door. On the porch were a couple of outdoor chairs and a small table. The view from here was of a small babbling brook that flowed close by, and the deep, moss covered greenery of the woods.

Inside there was a great room with an open floor plan. It contained a kitchen and a cozy living room. An overstuffed sofa and loveseat were set in front of a fireplace, while the kitchen had a small island that helped separate the space. It was complete with everything Scott would need, including a state-of-the-art coffee maker.

Through a doorway, Ross showed Scott the small office with a laptop that was networked with the one back at the estate. "Everything is backed up to a data center that my company owns. You'll never have to fear losing your work."

There was also a small bedroom with an en suite bathroom. "I figured if you ever got so engrossed in your novel and it got too late for you to come back to the main house, you could crash here for the night. Remember to let me know first, so I won't worry."

"This is amazing. Thank you so much, I love it! Is this why you had been pushing me to get back into my writing, Sir?"

"Well, it's one reason," Ross admitted, pulling Scott closer. "I also want to see you happy, sweetheart."

Scott leaned in and thanked him properly with a deep kiss.

"Mmm. The things you make me want to do to you ... shall we christen this cabin properly?"

Scott slid to his knees and looked up at him reverently. "Yes, Sir."

"That's my good boy. Get undressed and then look in that cabinet. I have a couple of surprises there for you."

A PROMISE FULFILLED

Scott removed his clothes, folding them neatly and placing them on top of the small dresser, before opening the cabinet. He grinned when he saw inside were three of his favorite implements, a paddle, a strap, and a belt.

"They're beautiful, Sir," Scott said as he ran his fingers over the leather of the strap.

"Pick one out and bring it to me," Ross instructed.

It took him a moment to decide, but Scott chose the strap. It was made of a beautiful fine-grain leather. Taking it, he closed the cabinet and brought it back to Ross.

"Now, choose where you want me to warm your ass. That's also where I'll be taking my pleasure from you."

A shiver ran through him and his cock twitched when an image came to his mind. His face felt flushed when he spoke. "The porch, Sir."

"I didn't know you had a thing for doing it outdoors," Ross teased.

"I ... I didn't either. It came to me when you asked, Sir."

"It's a good thing we're completely secluded out here," Ross said with a wink. "Go on, lead the way."

Scott made his way out toward the porch. Walking outside completely nude was both terrifying and freeing at the same time. His eyes darted around to make sure he didn't see anyone else before he let himself relax.

"Bend over the railing for me, sweetheart."

As he went to comply with the command, Scott's cock twitched in anticipation. Bending over the railing, he had a perfect view of the brook and woods. He felt even more vulnerable now that he couldn't see Ross or the cabin, but the solid railing he was bent over helped to ground him. The railing looked like it may even have been specifically designed for this activity in mind, being made from larger logs. The top of the railing was comfortable to bend over, almost like the spanking horse back in the playroom. *Ross planned that, didn't he?* Scott smirked to himself.

"What's your color?"

"Green, Sir. As green as all the moss growing on those trees."

"Good. You don't have permission to come from the strapping. I want to feel you peak when I'm buried deep inside you. If you come without permission, you'll be wearing the cock cage for a week."

Oh fuck. "Yes, Sir."

The strap began to fall rhythmically against his ass. The smacks echoed in the surrounding stillness as the stinging heat built up. Soon Scott's cock was hard and leaking, and he cried out with every new smack of the strap. The pain was too much and not enough. Scott could feel his balls draw up and he teetered on the edge of no return. "Yellow! Please ... I'm too close. I'm ... I don't want to earn a punishment. *Please, Sir?*"

"Good boy," Ross praised. Scott heard him put down the strap behind him. Next, he heard the distinct sound of a zipper before the cool feeling of lube dripped between his cheeks. "I'm going to open you up with my cock, nice and slow. Can you hold out a little longer, sweetheart?"

Taking a deep breath, he nodded. The edge of his impending orgasm had begun to recede. "Yes, Sir."

"Good. Once I start to speed up, you have my permission to come."

"Thank you, Sir."

"Your ass is so beautiful when it's bearing my marks," Ross praised, running his hands over the tenderized skin. "It turns such a beautiful shade of red."

The blunt head of Ross' cock began to tease its way into the cleft of Scott's ass. "What's your color now?"

"Green, Sir. *Please.*"

Slowly Ross began to rock his cock into his ass, teasingly slow. It felt like it took forever for the head to pop inside before he slowly worked the rest of the length in. Scott sobbed when Ross bottomed out and wrapped his arms around his chest.

Grasping the railing tightly, Scott savored every slow bump and grind that Ross gave him, making his own cock achingly hard. Ross began to pepper kisses up his neck as he kept making slow, shallow thrusts. Scott went weak in the knees when Ross began to kiss and suck marks into the side of his neck.

"You're always so good for me. Fuck, sweetheart. I love you so much," Ross growled into his ear.

Ross kept the slow grind going for a long time before he slowly raised himself and grasped Scott's hips tightly. From this new angle, Scott felt his prostate being hit with each thrust and he sobbed with relief as Ross began to fuck into him faster and harder.

Scott's cock was leaking steadily now as Ross thrust into him over and over. He canted his hips and met each thrust as he stopped holding back, letting the pleasure build up. He shamelessly cried out with each thrust, the sound echoing into the surrounding wilderness.

Soon the stimulation was too much, and Scott fell over the edge, letting himself go. His cock twitched and spurt all over the porch and railing as his vision went white.

Ross fucked him through it, slamming his hips hard against his tender ass. "Fuck, yes. You feel like a vice around my cock when you come."

When Scott came back to himself after his orgasm, he whimpered as Ross continued to fuck him hard. "Hush, be still and take it."

Gripping the railing hard, Scott held on while Ross continued to plow his ass, grunting and groaning behind him. A few moments later he thrust in hard and deep. Scott could feel Ross' cock twitch as he released pulse after pulse of his seed deep inside him.

Feeling Ross' release made his own cock twitch valiantly, despite being spent. Ross leaned back over, hugging him close. Twisting his head, Scott met Ross' lips as they shared a lingering kiss while Ross' cock continued to twitch inside of him.

"That was amazing, sweetheart," Ross said as he slowly slid out and turned Scott around to embrace him fully. "You have no idea how perfect you are for me."

Scott leaned back and smirked at him. "I think I have some inkling *by now*, Sir. I had no idea you were what I needed, but you're perfect for me, too."

* * *

They spent the rest of the day in the cabin making love. Ross took Scott again and again, until they were both completely sated. After a much-needed shower and a simple dinner, they decided it was too late to head back to the main house. Ross called his staff and informed them they were spending the night at the cabin.

Scott snuggled into Ross' arms as they settled into bed, letting out a happy sigh. "What are you thinking about?" Ross asked.

Shrugging, Scott replied. "I don't know, I guess the thought crossed my mind that right here, in your arms ... I'm home."

Ross squeezed his arms around him. "I'm happy to hear you say that. You've come a long way from when we first met."

"Yeah, I know. Looking back on it now ... I was so stupid ... yet..."

"Yet?"

Scott turned in Ross' arms, looking into his eyes in the dim light. "Well ... think about it. Would we have explored all these kinks together if you hadn't literally smacked some sense into me?"

Reaching up to caress his face, Ross shrugged. "You have a point, although ... I was into all this long before I met you. However, I would have introduced it to you a lot differently."

"Yeah, and I might not have been as open to trying it. Maybe we were fated to meet how we did, for our souls to align the right way?"

"I never thought of it that way before, but you could be right. Either way, I'm glad we did finally meet. You complete me in ways I never even dreamed imaginable."

"As do you ... *Sir*," Scott said as he leaned into Ross' caress. "I love you, Ross. You've left a permanent mark on my soul, and I wouldn't change that for anything."

"Neither would I, Scott. Neither would I."

Fin

ABOUT THE AUTHOR

Grayson Bell has been writing gay erotic romance stories since 2015. He identifies as a transgender man and is very invested in incorporating LGBTQ+ characters into his writing, and he loves exploring the love, romance, and intimacy that can occur between two men.

When he's not working on his stories, he loves playing video games, cooking, and spending time with friends.

Grayson on Amazon

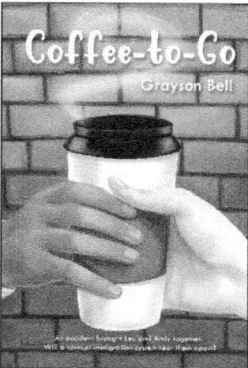

https://www.amazon.com/Grayson-Bell/e/B07H3B3D5G/

Other Works

Coffee-to-Go

A mutual love of coffee and an accident brought Leo and Andy together. Will a corrupt immigration system tear them apart?

For sale on Amazon!
http://www.amazon.com/dp/B07H32RCT2

Made in the USA
Monee, IL
28 April 2024

57659779R00152